Chapter 1

My eyes close. My body's sore, my spirit broken, and I wonder whether I have the strength or the inclination to carry on, knowing that I'm desperate to change my fate, that I need my happy ever after.

I'm woken suddenly by the radio alarm. The presenter's happy, lively voice fills the room with his morning flamboyance.

"Good morning, listeners. If you're just tuning in, it's 6 a.m. on this crisp, beautiful October morning, and, yes, someone has finally made an appearance in the sky. He's yellow, warm and making all the birds sing. So throw back the duvet and get up out of that lazy bed. It's Monday morning and the beginning of a brand-new week. And just to entice you a little more, here's the next track."

I yawn and stretch out my arms, opening my eyes to see him smiling at me with a hot coffee in his hands. I sit up in bed, tickled by the song that's playing, and he gives me a pleasant nod of his head.

"Good morning, Student Nurse Abigail." He grins as I reach out to him, taking my coffee. "Are you ready for your big day?"

I yawn again, sleepily taking a sip of my coffee, and murmur, "Hmm, my favourite."

I hear a thud and a little patter of feet. I grin to myself, knowing who this is.

"Brace yourself. Big fella's awake," he says with a smirk.

A very excited voice floods my ears as my little boy comes bounding into the bedroom.

"Mummy, Mummy, Mummy, look!" The quilt slips to one side and the bed starts to dip as he pulls himself onto the bed using the duvet as a rope, waving around his favourite toy by the ear – a small knitted rabbit. His eyes are wide. "Look, Mummy, look. It's Thump-Thump!" He's smiling at me, waiting for me to answer. I clear my throat and he laughs.

—

"Well, good morning, Thump-Thump. Good morning, you …"

He squeals, jumping up and down on the bed, hurling himself at me. We both giggle, and I grab him quickly and cuddle him tightly, kissing him on the cheek.

"Come on, big fella," his daddy says. "It's time to let Mummy get ready for her big day."

"Big-ga day?" he tries to say. I smile at him as my heart melts, feeling so much love for him.

"Yes, Angel," I reply, affectionately stroking the side of his face. "Big day for Mummy; first day on the wards today."

He's looking at me with a puzzled smile, not understanding what I'm saying. His daddy quickly snatches him off the bed and into his arms, nuzzling his chin into the side of our boy's neck, making him chuckle and filling the room with heartfelt laughter.

"Come on, big fella. Let's go and make Mummy some yum-yum."

He's still giggling and squirming in his daddy's arms, shouting excitedly, "And me and Thump-Thump." They both leave the room, leaving me laughing and alone, thinking about the day ahead.

6.30 a.m. The radio is still playing in the background – happy, feel-good songs – as I shower and dress in my uniform: a new stiff, starched white tunic top, navy trousers, and black flat shoes that have been polished to within an inch of their life; I can almost see my face in them. I finish my hair in a nice neat bun, secure it with clips, and apply a little light makeup before taking one last look in the mirror.

"Well, Abigail," I say out loud, "ready for it?" I hold a deep breath and think, Ready as I'll ever be.

6.35 a.m. I make my way down the stairs to the smell of scrambled eggs and toast, and I'm greeted by a happy voice and a beautiful smile.

"Breakfast is served, madam." He gestures with his hand towards the table, bowing slightly. I grin, looking at the table,

—

which is laid with a red rose, a good-luck card, scrambled eggs, wholemeal toast, coffee and fresh orange juice. He pulls out a chair, and as I sit down he lays a napkin on my knee. I smile, thinking, *How sweet – a napkin to save any spills on my new uniform*, because little things matter.

"Enjoy!" he says with an even bigger grin.

I thank him, still smiling, knowing I have the most kind, thoughtful and considerate man ever.

I sit at the table eating my breakfast, glancing out of the patio doors. A robin has caught my eye. It's sitting on the planter and chirping away proudly to itself. Its magnificent red breast is puffed out in all its glory.

He's noticed I'm looking at the robin and comments, "That's exactly how I feel today – proud."

"Proud?" I say, raising my eyebrows, puzzled.

"Yes, proud! Proud of you, Abigail." He winks. "Now eat your breakfast. It's getting cold."

Birds have now started to sing the dawn chorus in the garden as I eat my delicious scrambled eggs and hot, buttered toast. Oh, could this day get any better? I feel as though I'm in a beautiful dream.

6.50 a.m. I'm sitting in my car in the driveway. It's a beautiful car, polished and gleaming, and it smells new.

"Good luck, love!" he says as I hold my head out of the car window towards them both.

"Good duck, Mummy!" my son tries to mimic.

I kiss both my boys goodbye.

I smile. "See you tonight, and thank you!" I reply as I reverse out of the drive, seeing my son wriggling and waving in his father's arms, and I suddenly wonder, will I miss them?

6.55 a.m. The journey to the hospital is a breeze, and it's taking a lot less time than normal – all red lights turn green upon approach. Traffic is sparse, which is unusual for this time of morning as it's generally very busy. Parking at the hospital is no problem and I slide straight into a spot right next to the door. I walk over to the ticket machine and

—

discover a note on display.

All parking free for student nurses.

7.15 a.m. I'm early. I start making my way to the entrance of the hospital. As I enter the reception area, a round-faced porter in his late fifties greets me.

"Good morning, miss," he says in a clear voice. "Where may I direct you to this fine morning?"

I smile. "The Ear, Nose and Throat ward, please."

"Right, miss." He coughs, nods his head at me, and then continues, "Down the corridor, turn right, then second left, up one flight of stairs. At the top of the stairs go right, down the corridor, then second left ..." He nods his head at me again to confirm his directions. "And there you are, miss."

"Hmm. Sorry, can you say that again, please?" I reply, confused.

"Which bit?" he says, raising his eyebrows at me in amusement.

"All of it, please. Sorry!"

He looks away from me and over my shoulder, and I sense someone behind me. The porter stands a little straighter, pulling up his shoulders, and his voice is now clearer and louder.

"Good morning, Mr Black."

"Good morning, George," answers a beautiful voice from behind me. I turn to see who the owner is, as I vaguely recognise it. I gaze at him. He reminds me of someone, but I can't seem to place him. He looks mysterious; tall, dark and very handsome. It's a cliché, I know, but it's also true. Wow! To say he's a George Clooney-Brad Pitt lookalike doesn't even come close to describing this striking specimen of manhood. Three words instantly spring to my mind – God of Olympus – He's standing in front of me, around six feet two inches tall, dressed to kill in a designer suit. His eyes are drawing me in; they're a beautiful piercing green. I find myself unable to pull my gaze from them, and I think they look like kind eyes. They're absolutely captivating. I inhale and catch his scent; he

—

smells so fresh, like he's just walked through a field of newly mown grass. He really does remind me of someone, but I'm still unable to recall who it is.

I've spent a little too long admiring him. I feel my face starting to flush and I'm sure it's as red as a robin's breast, but then I think, *Why did I think of a robin?* I hear a child giggle loudly, and that giggle reminds me of something. I'm confused.

I breathe out, long and hard, as the porter announces, "This is one of yours, Mr Black. She's looking for your ward."

"Well," says Mr Black, "you'd better come with me so we can get you there on time."

I blush as I thank him, and I think nothing of going with him. We head off down the corridor. Mr Black turns to me while we're walking, looking at me as though he can read my thoughts.

"Sorry, I didn't catch your name."

"Abigail," I reply coyly, blushing and thinking, *Am I flirting with him?*

"Hmm, Abigail," he replies, rolling my name around his tongue. "It took me weeks to find my way around this hospital; it's like a rabbit warren."

I think about this for a second – as if rabbits mean something to me. He winks, then smiles, and that thought is immediately gone. His smile is dazzling, bright and wide, and it instantly reminds me of a toothpaste advertisement.

As we continue walking towards the ward, there are lots of nods of heads and Good morning, Mr Blacks, and it's evident that he's very high up in the hospital. Nurses avert their eyes as we walk past them, nudging each other, blushing and giggling like schoolgirls. He takes no notice of them and focuses on where he's going.

"Well, here we are. ENT. This is where I leave you. I'm off to head a conference call. Goodbye, Abigail. It was very nice to meet you and I'm looking forward to working with you soon."

"Goodbye, and it was very nice to meet you too!"

Mr Black heads towards an office with his name on the door.

I hold by breath, wondering what's going on inside my head.

7.25 a.m. I'm standing in the corridor of the ward, still trying to catch my breath. I'm confused and more than a little embarrassed by my reaction to him. A young woman immediately greets me, grinning like a Cheshire cat. As she introduces herself, she instantly reminds me of someone I know, jumping up and down, all hyperactive and eager to please.

"Hello!" she says, still smiling. "My name's Gail. I'm a student too. I've been allocated to show you around this morning, then take you into the handover. I see you've already met our resident hunk, Mr Black. Isn't he just dreamy?"

I close my eyes (Hmm! Mr Olympus) and smile at Gail, not really knowing what to say, but well aware that I'm blushing.

"This way."

Gail is so lively that she almost skips down the corridor; I almost have to run just to keep up with her. She shows me where to put my things, the staff toilets, staff room, and then takes me to the nursing office for the handover.

7.35 a.m. Gail opens the door and we enter the room. I follow behind her.

"Oh, good morning. Another angel has landed to join our flock," says a friendly voice.

"Good morning," I say, taken aback by the warm greeting.

"I'm Sister Bridget, and you must be Abigail." I like her instantly.

"Yes, I'm Abigail. Pleased to meet you," I reply, holding out my hand to shake hers. She returns the gesture, smiling favourably.

"Well, come on, my dear. Come and meet everybody."

—

The other nurses, around eight of them, come and introduce themselves to me, shaking my hand and saying, "Welcome to the Ear, Nose and Throat ward. We're all very pleased to meet you."

I'm dizzy by the time I've greeted everyone. I can feel a silly grin starting to spread across my face as I confess inwardly that I'm going to love working here.

7.45 a.m. "Okay," Sister Bridget says, "introductions over with. Let's hear the handover. Sister Hilary, if you would like to start, please."

Sister Hilary mentions each patient individually.

"Bed one." An in-depth report is given. She continues with beds two, three, four and five. She pauses. "And bed six is for theatre today." There's a sad expression on her face. "She was a little upset last night, so I read to her for about an hour."

"Oh, poor love," whispers a voice full of concern. Sister Hilary continues after nodding at the response from the other nurse.

"She's settled now, bless her. Beds seven, eight, nine and ten all had settled nights and are ready for discharge this morning after the ward round. Mr Black has asked that we all please join him for lunch today, as a way of saying thank you for all our hard work."

Several of the nurses make a swooning noise at the mention of his name. Gail goes as red as a beetroot, and my heart feels as if it's skipped a beat.

"Okay, okay, ladies," Sister Bridget says, smiling while shaking her head in amusement. "Thank you, Sister Hilary, for your handover. I'll see you tonight."

Sister Hilary nods her head at Sister Bridget, then starts making her way over to me as the other nurses are collecting their things. She shakes my hand again.

"Really nice to meet you, Abigail. I'm sure you'll love working here. I imagine we're going to be the best of friends."

"I'm sure I'll really love working here too, Sister Hilary.

And thank you."

As she's walking out of the room, I sense a kindness and sincerity about her, as if nothing would ever be too much trouble or effort. She's a genuine, lovely person, one you would want as a friend.

As I think this, Sister Bridget claps her hands and says in a clear, but gentle way, "Okay, angels, go and do your magic!" As everyone starts to leave the room, she turns to me. "Abigail, you'll be working alongside me today. I've just got a few things to collect from the nurses' station. Would you wait here for me, please, dear? Help yourself to tea or coffee if you wish. It's over on the table." She points in the direction of the coffee table. "It's fresh, and I won't be long."

"Okay, thank you."

She smiles warmly towards me, then leaves the room.

The staff room is now empty and quiet. I do pour myself a coffee and sit in one of the comfortable armchairs. After about five minutes, I start reading the notice board.

Charity Ball, 31st October, in aid of the Children's Hospice, 7 p.m. start. All welcome, students free.

Staff Meeting, 8 a.m. and 8 p.m. 4th October.

Student of the Month Award. Awarded to Heather, ENT. Well done! Heather wins a two-week all-inclusive holiday to Mauritius for four people.

Gosh, that's fantastic! You can win a holiday every month? This all sounds too good to be true. I feel like a kid in a candy shop who's just been told to choose whatever I want, and that stupid grin has appeared on my face again. Maybe I'll be like Gail at the end of the day – all hyperactive and giddy. Is this place for real? I've heard of dream jobs before, but I never thought I'd land one. Well, not one like this.

I start humming to myself, smiling as I do so. I've read the notice board twice, and I'm now on my second cup of coffee. I stand up, too excited to sit, and hum happy tunes to myself. I notice a radio on the coffee table, and I suddenly want to sing out loud. I don't think I've ever felt so happy. I press the on

—

9

button, but instead of a happy song I hear a man singing about how bad life is, about killing people and shooting children in a playground. My face drops and my mood changes abruptly as I pull in my lip. I don't want to listen to this. I quickly press the button to change the channel, but it's the same song. I blurt out, "No!" I press different buttons repeatedly, but the song is on every station. That's not right – it can't be on every station.

A voice sniggers then mutters, "That'll teach you, bitch."

I'm momentarily shocked, but I now recognise who it is. But what is he doing here? My heart picks up speed and my eyes flicker. The snigger fills the room and I desperately want to keep my eyes closed and stay in my dream just a little longer. But I can't. I have to open them to reality.

Chapter 2

I'm baffled as I stare at the clock; it's 6.30 a.m. but the alarm hasn't gone off, and I swear to God that I set it. I fly out of bed feeling panicked, knowing that I'm going to be late, and on my first day. Adam's leaving the bedroom. He hasn't spoken, although he's still sniggering. I glare at his back. I hate him so much that I want to throw the alarm clock at the back of his head, but I daren't. I start to mumble under my breath as I'm getting out of bed, because I'm damn certain he's turned my alarm off.

"Spiteful, horrible man."

He hears me and starts to turn around, his tone smug and nasty as always.

"Something to say, Abbie?"

I take a deep breath, not answering, hoping that I've not fuelled another argument, knowing what will happen if I have. Surprisingly, he ignores me and walks out of the door. Then I remember that he has meeting today and he'll not want to be late, although he shouts back at me, just as he's leaving, "I'll fucking deal with you tonight, and we'll discuss this again – you starting a new job."

I close my eyes, knowing this has to stop. Discuss this new job? We discussed it last night, and because I said no to him, because I insisted that I was starting my new job, he hit me.

I run to the bathroom, nervous, knowing he's downstairs and brewing for a showdown tonight. I wash and dress in my new uniform. I apply a little makeup, but don't make a very good job of it because my hands won't stop shaking. I'm nervous about him and the thought of having to come back home tonight to face the music. I should be happy and excited to tell my husband over a meal at the table about the day I've had, what I've learnt and the friends I've made, but instead I'll come back to a slanging match, to the banging and slamming of doors. And if he wants to hit me, he will. Then he'll drink too much, as always, and demand … I shudder, wiping that thought straight out of my head.

I grit my teeth and try to put on my shoes and fasten them without falling down the stairs. I'm absolutely livid as I grab my bag and books.

I'm about to run down the stairs when I catch sight of myself in the mirror. I adjust the collar on my uniform, pulling it up slightly to cover the bruise on the back of my neck. I look tired, and I've lost too much weight from the sleepless nights and endless arguing. I've not eaten properly for months because of all that's happened, all the things that Adam has done. He's drained my soul. How did I allow myself to be deceived by him?

At first, he was charming and kind, but now he's a monster. I'm desperate to leave him, but I'm struggling. I've nowhere to go and he'll not leave. And I finally know the real reason he married me – it wasn't for love; it was my money, and I think the past four years have all been a sham. I shake my head at my reflection.

One more thing, and I know it will tip me over the edge.

I lift my eyes, remembering my dream, and what a lovely dream it was. I want my life to be like that dream, but it's not. It's a nightmare – a nightmare I'm desperately trying to escape from. I screw my eyes tightly shut, my hand over my belly, but there's nothing there any more, just an empty shell. Like me – an empty shell of the person I used to be.

I need to get out of this rut. Look at me, brainwashed and defenceless.

I mutter, "Yes, Adam. No, Adam. Three bags full, Adam."

Too many years of being controlled? I take a deep breath and begin walking quietly down the stairs. Then I head down the hallway towards the front door, not wanting Adam to hear me. I've neither the inclination nor strength to argue with him this morning, to be told what to do or what to wear, and I know he'll try to stop me from leaving the house if I give him half a chance.

I walk quickly through the front door towards my car, taking out my keys from my bag as I go. I open the car door and get inside, setting the key into the ignition and turning it. Nothing happens. I try again. Still nothing.

I scream at the car, "Start, you —" The engine starts with a bang. I jump, knowing he's bound to have heard. I'm starting to feel scared and flustered, knowing I'm disobeying him, and that I'll pay for doing so.

I start to reverse my car off the drive, but I have to stop as Mr Blake is walking past with his dog. I'm willing him to be quick before Adam realises I've gone, but he appears at the front door. He's dressed for work, wearing a black suit, pale-blue shirt and blue tie. I muster a half-smile, not wanting to antagonise him. His face is set and I know what's coming, but it suddenly changes as he sees Mr Blake. He nods towards him, smiling.

"Morning, Jack."

"Morning, Adam. A beautiful day."

"Yes, I love these crisp, sunny October mornings."

"Abigail seems in a rush this morning. I shouted to her, but she dashed into her car. I don't think she heard me. Is she starting at the hospital? I noticed the uniform." Adam smiles, nodding his head, but he glares at me. "You must be so proud of her, Adam. You've got it all, mate; a beautiful wife, house, car. You don't know how lucky you are."

Mr Blake nods at me in the car, and I'm willing him to shut up and just go home. Adam stares at me, then smiles back at Mr Blake.

"Yes, I have. Aren't I the lucky chap?" And I hear the cynicism in his voice.

I want to vomit, listening to them both, looking at Adam standing there. How can he?

"Well, I'd better get in. Marmalade will want her breakfast. See you for the football on Saturday."

"Maybe, although I might be away on business this weekend."

I close my eyes. Maybe? Oh, I hope that was just a slip of the tongue. I've made arrangements to see my gran at the weekend and it's the only thing I've got to look forward to. I can't go if he's at home – he'll not let me.

"Okay, just let me know, mate." He smiles at me, raising his hand. "Bye, Abigail. Good luck with the new job!"

I just nod towards him as he moves out of the way and starts heading towards his house with his dog. I take my chance and carry on reversing while Adam's watching Mr Blake leave. He glares at me, warning me as I'm backing out of the drive, but I know he'll not say anything in front of our neighbour. He doesn't want to spoil his reputation or his standing in the community.

To look at him, standing there, smiling, nodding his head, his blonde hair immaculately cut, large blue eyes, designer suits, flash car, tanned, tall, toned body, perfect straight white teeth, he has all the appearance of the boy next door. But he's not the boy next door. I honestly don't know who he is.

Yes, I do. He's a monster. He's the original Jekyll and Hyde.

He has never said a bad word to me in front of anyone: it all happens behind closed doors.

He throws his hands up into the air, miming something at me through gritted teeth. I know he's really angry, and I can imagine the words he just mouthed, but then he turns and goes back inside, slamming the door shut behind him. My heart is pounding.

I'm so glad he's gone indoors. I hate him. We don't talk much, well not at all. He just shouts at me all the time. But I have started to answer him back, and this infuriates him. I've started to stand up for myself a little.

I'm not as timid as I used to be, although his temper and drinking have gotten worse over the past six months. It's horrible. And, as always, I find myself walking on egg shells because of his moods and his free use of his fists on me.

Like last night. I know I'll pay dearly for that tonight, for ignoring him. I know deep down inside that I shouldn't have done it, but I have, and I can't do anything about it now. I wish to God I had a bit more courage, that I could stick up for myself. I manage to do it with other people. I feel like I'm living two lives – Abbie, who smiles at the right times, laughs at the right times, even says the right things at the right times, just so people don't get an idea of what my life is really like with Adam. Then there's Abigail. My secret self. My life with Adam, one I never speak about to anyone. I'm too ashamed of myself for putting up with what he's done to me. I used to be quite independent before I met him, but now I'm a shadow of my former self, living this mundane life. I'm quiet and obedient, I nod and smile, and I'm constantly saying yes or sorry to save …

I huff, muttering to myself, "To save what?"

I don't know any more, although I'm sick of living like this. I'd rather take a beating, his abuse, than continue my life with him.

I have decided, though, that I am going to leave him. I'm just biding my time, waiting for the right moment, and he knows I'm changing. I've become defiant, he said. Doing as I please, answering back. He tried to hit it out of me, but I took the punches, knowing, or hoping, that there was finally a light at the end of the tunnel.

My phone rings in my bag, and I know it's him, but I don't answer it, not this time, not like I used to, because I know what he'll demand from me – to turn round and go home. And for what? A beating? Shouting? Continuing to be controlled? No.

I drive down the road in a daze, thinking about what I've just said and done, robotically turning left at the bottom of the road, and not even realising that the lights are on red. I drive through them in a dream to join the busy main road. A horn blasts, startling me and making me jump in my seat. It brings me quickly to my senses as I hit my screeching breaks and scream.

"Oh shit!"

Straight ahead of me is a brand-new black BMW sports car, and driving it is a very angry, aggressive, dark-haired man in a suit. He looks furious. I hear another blast of a horn, and he has to swerve out of the way of another driver approaching from up the road.

Oh God, I'm going to hit him.

I want to close my eyes, but I can't. My heart is racing, and my hands are shaking so much that I struggle to hold on to the steering wheel. My car comes to an abrupt, screaming halt, jolting me forward and then back again into my seat. He pulls his window down, shaking his head. I'm in shock, shouting, "Sorry, sorry, sorry." I close my eyes briefly, breathing fast, but relieved I've not hit him. I reopen them slowly and cautiously, and Mr BMW is glaring at me.

He looks furious as he yells, "You stupid bloody woman. Your lights were on red. Are you blind?"

He continues shouting and swearing at me, and I'm praying he doesn't get out of his car.

I start to put down the window and reply, "I'm sorry." My voice is unsteady, but he carries on verbally abusing me. I shout a little louder. "I'm sorry! God, no harm done. How many more times?"

He shakes his head and gives me a hand gesture. My eyes go wide and I'm equally unamused, so I repeat the same generous gesture back at him, making a clenched fist and moving it towards my forehead, pulling it back and forth as he'd done. He's glaring at me, his lips pulled in tight as he reaches for his seatbelt.

Shit, I think. *He's getting out.* I start my engine quickly and drive forward, moving to the side of his car, blocking his door. He's livid, and I'm bloody annoyed now.

I poke my tongue out, pulling a face at him, shouting as I drive past, "You Richard Cranium."

His eyes are wide, and he's not amused. He feeds me the finger, so I give him a dirty look as I drive past him. "BMW

---

drivers," I huff. "They think they own the bloody road."

I check my mirror to see if he's following me, but he's still on the main road, shaking his head in disbelief. He's really pissed off and clearly has no sense of humour, but who could blame him? It was my fault, after all. I shrug my shoulders, letting out a deep sigh. I had been a little hasty, but there'd been no need for him to behave like that. I mutter quietly to myself, "Dickhead."

I check my fob watch; it's now 7.05 a.m. Great, my nerves are shot to pieces, and if I make it to the hospital on time and not via A&E, it will be a bloody miracle.

I continue on my journey, paying a lot more attention to my driving, but I'm in a worse mood now than I was when I set off. I feel nervous and jumpy. Every light is on red, and every driver is out to get me. Even the Sunday drivers are on the road, the flat-cap brigade.

"Great, a bloody tractor." It's pulled out right in front of me, driving at one mile an hour. I sigh. Could this morning get any worse?

I eventually pull into the hospital car park, and it's full. I check the time – 7.35 a.m. *Come on, Abbie. Think.* I see a space on a small grass verge. I'll have to; I've no choice. I reverse my car on to it and grab my bag and books off the back seat.

I notice my trainers and running things next to them, and it jolts my memory to ring Joe and tell him I've started, all thanks to him. I've not seen him for weeks. Adam put a stop to me going to the running club when he found out about my new job, saying it was obvious I was meeting people who swayed me into making my own decisions. Joe can't contact me. I didn't dare give him my number because of Adam.

I leave my car on the grass verge, not really giving a damn if they tow it. I want this job – I need it – and I won't be late on my first day.

I run up the incline of the car park towards the entrance of the hospital and the heavens open. I'm soaking wet by the time I reach the top, but I stop and look up at the sign. Saint

Mary's Hospital.

"Thanks Joe," I say quietly, and I wonder if I'll see him today. I take a long, deep breath. My tummy is churning with butterflies, but I'm also a little proud of myself, knowing I've done it. I hold my hands together, and take another deep breath. And now for my false smile. Some women never leave home without their lipstick, others tissues, but not me. I never leave home without my false smile.

I'm very aware of the time as I run into the reception area. I've about ten minutes if I don't want to be late. I start running hell for leather down the corridor towards the lifts, skidding to a halt as I notice a sign on the lift door. *Out of order.* I roll my eyes. Brilliant, and only four flights to go. I'm going to be late.

I start running up the stairs, and by the time I've reached the top I'm hyperventilating, sweating, and my pulse must be around a hundred and forty beats per minute. At least I've made it to the doorway of the ward without passing out. I catch sight of myself in the key pad. God, I look a mess.

I press the call button, messing with my hair and trying to make it presentable, wiping under my eyes to remove the mascara that's run.

A voice answers: "Hello, can I help you?"

I open my mouth, but nothing comes out. I can hardly breathe.

"Hello, hello, can I help you?"

Oxygen, I want to say, but I still can't find my voice. She must know the lift's not working. I press the button again.

"Hello?"

I manage to find the last bit of oxygen buried deep in my lungs, and answer, "Student nurse."

She buzzes me in.

I'm on the ward and someone is shouting at me.

"Come on! You only have five minutes until handover and Sister gets really cross if she's kept waiting. Come on! Come on! Oh, by the way, I'm Alison, another student. What's your name?"

Alison is extremely hyperactive, jumping up and down, shouting at me.

"Come on, come on, you don't want the wrath of Sister, do you?" She pauses, looking at me, and asks again – because I've not said – "What's your name?"

I take a deep breath and think before I speak, not wanting to say something to offend her. I simply reply, "Abigail."

"Pleased to meet you, Abigail. Come on, quick. I'll show you where to put your things." She grabs my hand, and starts running me down the corridor, towards what I can make out is the staff room. Oh, my sweet Lord in heaven, no! Please, it's the girl from my dream. Why could I not have had him instead?

I dump my things on the staff-room floor and check the time. 7.44 a.m. I follow Alison into another room with a sign that reads *Staff Only*. There're chairs around a coffee table, and at the far end is a bed and some cupboards, like a treatment area. It's not what I had imagined, I think, walking into the room, disturbing the handover, which has already begun.

A stern-looking woman greets us, glaring over rounded spectacles. Her uniform is a navy dress, secured around the middle with a black elastic belt with a huge silver nursing buckle. She's slender, her black hair scraped back into a bun from which not one hair escapes, and she's probably in her late fifties. This is Sister. She's scary. Unlike in my dream, the rest of the staff look hostile towards me too.

Sister taps her watch with a pointed finger, shouting at us both.

"Late?" she bellows. "I will not tolerate lateness, nor will I tolerate shoddiness," she continues in a hostile voice. "Get a piece of paper from the table, take out your pens and sit down."

My eyes are like saucers. God, is she going to give us lines?

"Write down your handover. Do not speak. And if you

---

don't understand something then I suggest you go away and research it. I'm not your babysitter, I am the Sister. I am in charge of this ward and I do not suffer fools gladly," she barks.

Hell, I've joined the bloody army. I sit very still, trying my best not to move or breathe.

She continues. "Right, listen up; Bed one, laryngectomy patient. Mrs Baker, forty-five years old. Private side, Ward one. Back from theatre Saturday night. Post-op thirty-six hours. Drains are still in-situ. The PEG hasn't been sited yet."

Whispering immediately starts in the room, and one nurse, rolling her eyes, asks a little abruptly, "And why has the peg not been sited, Sister?"

I look at the nurse who has just asked the question, and everyone is muttering in the room.

Sister shouts, "Silence!" Every nerve in my body jumps, making me drop my paper and pen. The pen rolls under the table and I bend down to get it as she continues, "Have you quite finished?"

I daren't look at her. Does she mean me? I look up and she's glaring at me. This woman is so scary.

"Sorry," I say timidly, sitting back in my chair and leaving my paper and pen on the floor.

"One more interruption and I'll ask you to leave. Can I continue?" she remarks sarcastically.

I don't respond. Instead I nod, sitting bolt upright in my chair, staring at her and willing her to continue with the handover so that everybody will stop looking at me. I feel like a naughty child.

"She's been experiencing tachycardia rhythms most of the night. BP elevated, O2 de-humidified via a facemask in-situ over the stoma site, running at ten per cent, suction given regularly, hourly observation and close monitoring required. Dressings to be changed today. And if anyone has any further remarks to make about the care of Mrs Baker then they can bring them up with Mr Scott, who will be in shortly."

She'd said all that in one breath and had completely lost me after drains in-situ. Hell, what am I doing here? I have no idea what all that meant. Was she even speaking English? And that was just bed one. Surely I can't be expected to look after these patients. I'm in way over my head. Where are all the patients who need Strepsils, paracetamol, and cough medicine? This place is like a different planet.

I'm brought suddenly out of my state of panic as the door opens, and I notice that Sister's voice has changed as she greets the person entering.

"Mr Scott!"

There's a silence in the room, and I don't imagine anyone is breathing. You could hear a pin drop.

"Have you come to hand over bed one?" Her voice is different, soft and almost human. I look at her, puzzled. What could possibly have melted the hard exterior of this woman? Then it dawns on me. It's obvious that she has a massive crush on Mr Scott. All eyes turn towards the doorway, and I slowly turn my head to see what everyone is looking at. My heart skips a beat. I'm in shock, speechless, and a host of strange feelings start to flood my body and mind. I feel myself start to panic. Oh, this cannot be happening.

A voice in my head confirms: *Oh, Abigail, but it is.*

I reply silently, "Please no. Why me?"

Chapter 3

I'm staring towards the door at a dark-haired man in a suit. He's about six feet tall, handsome, oozing authority and power, and wearing a not-so-pleasing smile on his face. His eyes survey the room, and stop at mine. He looks stumped at first, but then his eyes go wide as he recognises me. Now he looks annoyed.

Oh dear Lord, why is this happening now? I'm squirming in my seat. I want a big hole to appear and swallow me up.

He speaks in a clear and authoritative voice. "I'm sorry I'm late, Sister. I was almost run off the road this morning by a lunatic driver with a very clever mouth."

My eyes close, my face flushes, and I'm wishing now that I'd not acted so hastily.

Sister merely shakes her head at every word he says, remarking sympathetically, "People like that shouldn't be on the road."

Everyone in the room agrees with her with a round of *oohs* and *ahs*, and gasps of sympathy. He nods, an agreeable expression on his face, as though they're all his allies.

I feel slightly intimidated as his eyes are still firmly fixed on mine, though now they look amused at my discomfort. I realise that he's enjoying this.

Sister is still sucking up to him, and she carries on in the most pathetic voice I've heard in a long while. "They should bring back the birch, horse whip them." There's a murmur of agreement. "Did you know the person responsible, Mr Scott?" she says, all sweetness and light.

"No," he remarks with a raised eyebrow. My heart is racing. I want to leave, but I don't. His voice is sarcastic. "And they clearly didn't know me" – his eyes move briefly to Sister's, then return to mine – "as they called me Richard."

A little noise leaves my throat, but the room is so silent that it sounds like a screech, and everyone turns to look at me. I quickly pull my lips in tight, but I'm thinking of the irony of calling him a Richard Cranium. I stop suddenly, noticing Sister's face.

"Do you find this amusing, Nurse Baxter?"

I stare at her and shake my head, but she continues to glare back at me. I can feel everyone's eyes on me. I'm so embarrassed. I'm not sure what's wrong with me, behaving like this. It's not like me – what I did this morning, what I said to him, or what I've done just now. I move my eyes from hers to his. I'm about to speak, but find his stare overpowering me, so when I say nothing Sister shouts at me again.

"Well?"

I suddenly feel warm and flushed. I try to swallow so that I can answer her, but my throat is really dry. I try to sit forward, but instead I find myself swaying, and all the while I'm looking at him, looking at me. Everyone in the room is staring at me, with the exception of Sister, who's staring at him.

Whoa! I think, and I'm pretty sure I'm going to be sick. The room starts to spin, and I try to compose myself. Why do I feel like this? I'm going to pass out. I need to leave, but as I try to stand I begin to sway, and I hear a voice in the distance.

"Oh, Abigail! Oh my God, look at her head and all the blood." I'm confused and dazed. Blood? What's happening?

I hear another voice, a man's.

"I've got her. I'll sort this, Sister. You get everyone out and to work."

Sister hollers, making me wince, her voice hurting my head. I think I might have passed out.

"You heard Mr Scott. Everybody out. All of you, get to work." Sister's hanging back, continuing, "Do you want me to help you, Mr Scott?"

"No, I'm fine. You can leave too, Sister," he says as he bends over me.

I struggle to get up from the floor, but I feel strange and my head hurts. I rub my lips together, tasting blood in my mouth. I hear the door open and people talking as they leave, but I can't make out what they're saying. Then the door closes, and we're alone. He's kneeling beside me, speaking softly.

"Let me help you." He places one arm around my waist and the other under my legs, picking me up from the floor like I'm a child and carrying me towards the bed at the far end of the room. I squint at the lights; they're hurting my eyes, and my head.

I feel confused and embarrassed, so I snap, "I'm fine. Please, put me down."

His reply is firm. "And I said, let me help you."

I feel his breath on the side of my face, and it sends a shiver down my spine. He's holding me close to him, his hand around my waist resting gently on my tummy. He looks at me, and I feel my face flush suddenly. I look away quickly, not understanding what I'm feeling. He sits me on the bed, and now that I'm face to face with him my heart is racing. I bite my bottom lip as he moves in close to me, scooping my legs up in one arm, twisting me so that my legs are on the bed and pushing my shoulders backwards, forcing me to lie down, speaking firmly as he does so.

"Lie down and let me look at your head."

I watch him, confused, still feeling strange and dizzy. I lie back on the bed and he moves my hair from my face, shaking his head as I wince at the pain. He moves away, out of sight, but I can hear him behind me opening and closing drawers, placing things onto a tray. He returns, speaking clearly and firmly. "I'm just going to clean the wound for you."

I feel flustered. I don't really know what's happened. My reply is a little muddled.

"The wound?"

"Yes. You fainted and caught your head on the side of the coffee table. It's quite a nasty cut."

I don't answer him, but I start to remember everything: his performance in the handover, what happened this morning with Adam, and, of course, the altercation with him before I started work today. Is it any wonder I fainted? I look

---

at him and begin to recall more of his behaviour during the handover. No, that's why I fainted, because of his smug arrogance, and how he made me feel in front of everyone. It was humiliating.

He's placed something cold on my head and I wince, moaning softly.

"Ouch!"

I move my head to stop the smarting. His voice is stern, as if he's telling off a small child.

"Keep still."

I let out a large sigh, wanting to reply, but I'm a little taken aback by his last comment. He ignores me and continues cleaning the wound, before saying in a matter of fact tone. "It doesn't need stitches. These will do." He places some strips over the cut, and then a dressing. "I'll get you something for the pain. Stay here on the bed." He raises his voice, just a little. "And don't move."

He turns, leaving the room.

I'm left alone, feeling confused and a little intimidated by him. My uniform feels wet. I take a look and see that it's soaked with my blood. I frown, questioning why I didn't speak back to him. I'm normally more vocal than that, but my head is throbbing, and I still feel a little dizzy and sick.

I jump as the door opens, expecting him to walk back through, but instead a nurse enters abruptly and glares at me, huffing and puffing, and throwing me daggers. I remember seeing her at the handover; she was the one who asked the question about the PEG and got shouted at by Sister. She doesn't speak to me, but walks over to the drawers and starts banging around, throwing things into the bin. She turns and walks out of the room, slamming the door hard behind her. I stare at the closed door, wondering what's going on.

The door opens again, and I'm not sure who to expect this time.

It's Mr Scott, wearing a conceited look on his face, and holding a pill pot in one hand and a glass of water in the other. I think he's very handsome, but I also think he knows that. He's cocky and arrogant, and at that moment I've taken an instant dislike to him. I don't speak. He stands beside of me, and his presence in the room is overwhelming. He's overbearing and very confident. Too confident for my liking. He's annoying me with that smug expression of his, shaking the medicine pot in front of my face so that the pills rattle inside. Even more irritating is the way he's speaking to me with a hint of amusement in his voice, as if he finds the way I'm glaring at him funny.

"Open."

I frown at him.

His expression changes and his voice is suddenly stern. "Do as you're told."

I pull in my lips and hold my hand out instead. He raises an eyebrow. There's a slight smirk on his face as he puts the pills into my hand.

He goes to put the glass to my mouth, but I shake my head and reply firmly, "I can manage, thank you."

I reach out to take the glass, and as I do our fingers touch. An electric pulse shoots through me, jolting my nervous system, and I feel my face flush. He's staring at me, and he's noticed the blush creeping across my cheeks. I snatch my hand away, embarrassed, and try to rationalise what's just happened. I put the pills into my mouth and take a sip of the water. I can sense him still looking at me, even though I can't bring myself to look at him. I feel my face going redder. My heart picks up speed. He takes the glass from my hand and we touch again. I feel the same surge of electricity flooding my veins, and I'm praying that my hands don't start shaking. I close my eyes and try to dismiss these feelings, but when I open them I find him watching me, and I can sense an intense chemistry between us. He speaks, his voice firm.

"The pills will help with the pain. Get some rest, and don't get up."

God, my head is all over the place, but he's so imperious

towards me that I suddenly find myself annoyed again. Who does he think he is? I know he's my boss, but, bloody hell, are there no boundaries? Do I have to do as he tells me? This isn't work related, not really. I'm about to say something when he abruptly turns and leaves the room.

The door closes with a bang, and I lie on the bed muttering to myself, "What the hell is happening to me?"

I sigh and close my eyes, feeling drowsy and immensely confused by why I'm thinking and behaving like this. My mind is drifting and I can't seem to settle for thinking about Mr Scott. My heart thuds as I remember how I felt when our fingers touched. I'm desperately trying to convince myself that it's nerves, and just a very bad start to the day. I eventually fall asleep, totally baffled.

I'm woken by voices outside the room, people talking and asking questions.

"Why is the staff room closed?"

"I believe a student had an accident in there this morning, and she's still in there, recuperating."

"Oh," replies another voice. "So where's the handover then?"

"I think at the nursing station."

"Right, come on then. We don't want to be late for Sister, do we?"

They laugh as they walk away. I don't know how long I've slept. I open my eyes and focus on the room. I'm a little light-headed, but I feel warm and notice that a blanket's been placed over me. I check under the blanket to see if I'm still wearing my uniform, but then I catch myself and feel a little stupid. This is a hospital, after all, and I'm perfectly safe here. I put my hand to my head, flummoxed. I catch the wound and moan.

Ouch, that hurts.

The door opens, and Mr Scott walks in. He's gorgeous, but he's also arrogant and bossy. He smiles at me, and I'm annoyed to feel myself blush. His voice is soft as he walks over to me.

"How are you feeling now, Abigail?"

My voice is quiet, almost a whisper.

"Umm …" I pause. "My head's still very sore."

He steps closer, and my pulse starts to race. Again, I'm baffled by my feelings. I try to sit up, but my head swims as the room starts to spin. He rushes to me, grabbing me before I fall from the bed, holding me in his arms, close to his chest, his body touching mine. He smells so nice and fresh, and I'm suddenly getting feelings, impulses, that I know I shouldn't have towards him. I tell myself to stop, but I can't seem to stop my body from reacting this way. I don't like him, but I can't seem to get these thoughts of him out of my head.

I stare at him, and think that he must know what is going on in my mind. He's looks down at me, and I notice for the first time how beautiful his eyes are. They remind me of fresh blades of spring grass blowing gently in a breeze. They're so inviting that I can't stop looking at them. His lashes are dark and long, and when he blinks I feel as if they're beckoning me. He smiles, and I blush, knowing that I'm staring. I try my best to pull my gaze away, but his eyes are entrancing. He's holding me so tightly that I can feel the rapid beat of his heart. My head starts to spin again. The room has suddenly grown too warm, and beads of sweat form on my brow. My mouth has gone dry. He's still looking at me, his expression concerned.

"Are you okay? You've gone very pale."

He moves his arms, pulling away from me to survey the situation. Without any warning, I suddenly throw up, splattering his trousers. My face is rigid with shock.

"I'm sorry … I'm so sorry."

His expression is stunned at first as he reaches for a towel.

"Are you okay?" he asks again.

I nod in response, and he simply nods back at me. Then his expression quickly changes to one of puzzlement – like he's pondering something before he speaks.

"Was that totally necessary?" he says, sounding unsure as he wipes his trousers. He pauses, a half-smile on his face like he's laughing at me. Then, with a raised eyebrow, he adds inquisitively, "Or were you aiming for my trousers?"

I can feel my jaw drop – did he really just say that? I'm dumbstruck, and even more so when, very slowly and suggestively, he drops the towel and moves his hand towards the buckle on his belt. My eyes are as wide as saucers.

He wouldn't, surely?

He watches me, waiting for a reaction, but all I can do is stare at him in astonishment. Oh, my sweet Lord in heaven, this cannot be happening.

Amused by my reaction, he grins widely, speaking with a hint of laughter in his voice. "Was it your intention to get me naked from the waist down?"

I make a garbled noise in my throat.

"No, no it … it wasn't."

"Really?" He sighs, tilting his head to one side. "Are you sure about that?"

Bloody hell, I think. He's goddamn mad. I've heard some chat-up lines before but, hell, that was a classic. I have a sudden overwhelming urge to laugh, although I have no idea why, because I think he's playing me. We're interrupted by a knock at the door. I jump, trying to get up off the bed. Whoa! I'm still dizzy, and the room starts to spin. I misplace my hand and fall from the bed. Sprawled on the floor, I look up at him. He looks surprised, but also amused as he walks over to me. He bends down and I think he's going to help me up, but instead he moves his lips towards my ear, and his words linger softly.

"Umm, nice. I love a new position."

I gape at him. I can't believe he's just said that. I find myself wondering if he really is a surgeon at all, or some crazed lunatic who's just wandered in off the street to impersonate a doctor. I can't believe that someone of his status is behaving like this. He holds out his hand to help me up, but

I shake my head and refuse the gesture.

He's crazy, I think, as he rolls his eyes at me, shouting, "Come in."

The door opens and Sister walks in. Never would I have thought I'd be so pleased to see her.

"Is everything all right, Mr Scott?" she asks, puzzled as she notices me on the floor.

He answers her sharply. "Fine, why shouldn't it be?" She looks surprised, as he continues in an authoritative tone. "Sister, Abigail has had an accident." He looks at me and grins, raising both eyebrows. She hasn't noticed, and he looks down towards his trousers, shaking his head. I can't quite believe how he's conducting himself. Sister seems shocked as well. Her face is flushed, and she coughs in embarrassment.

"May I get you some clean trousers, Mr Scott?" She sounds nervous.

"No, I'm fine. Abigail will need to stay in hospital overnight to be monitored. She has concussion. Put her in one of the private side rooms."

"Not the Medical Admissions Unit?"

"No," he replies sharply. "If I meant MAU, I would have said MAU. I said a private side room. Are you quiet clear on that, Sister?"

She goes red again, and looks chastised.

Where did that come from? It's obvious he doesn't like to be questioned.

My voice, when I speak, is soft. "Is it really necessary for me to stay in hospital? I'm sure I'll be fine at home."

He turns and looks at me. "Yes, it is necessary."

Sister stares at us both, her eyes darting between us as if she can't quite believe what's happening.

"Sister, help Abigail off the floor and transfer her to a private side room immediately."

I look at him, stunned. I don't know whether to argue back or keep my mouth shut. I look at Sister, but there's no help to be had from her. I feel like I'm in an episode of the

Twilight Zone. I decide to speak, although my voice is quiet.

"I need to let Adam know that I'm staying in hospital." Mr Scott doesn't say anything so I carry on, feeling suddenly nervous. "If I'm not home then he'll ..." I pause, thinking quickly of something else to say other than the truth. *He'll beat the living daylights out of me.* "He'll ... he'll ring my gran if I'm not home. She'll panic, and I don't want her to get upset."

"And who is Adam?" he barks.

I take a deep breath, rolling my eyes at the thought of him. "He's my husband."

Disappointment flashes across his face, as he shakes his head.

"Sister can do that," he snaps, and we both jump at his tone.

I don't understand why he seems so angry, but Sister responds immediately and nods her head.

"Yes, yes, Mr Scott. I'll ring her husband."

She lingers on the word husband, just for a moment. He turns abruptly and walks towards the door, but stops at the last moment and looks back at me. He glares at me, tight-lipped, shaking his head. He doesn't say anything as he opens the door and walks out, slamming it shut behind him. I jump again, and the bang of the door vibrates around my head, making it throb. I stare at the closed door, wondering what the hell has just happened. Moreover, I wonder what the hell is happening to me.

Chapter 4

Sister walks over to me, shaking her head. She doesn't speak, but gives me a withering look and holds out her hand reluctantly as she sees me trying to pull myself up from the floor using the bed. There's little sympathy in her gesture.

My legs are wobbly and my head is pulsating, but I'm thankful that she's not talking – I don't think I could take her voice screeching at me right now; I'm sure my head would explode.

But I've thought too soon.

"Follow me," she snaps.

I cringe. My head feels like it's being crushed in a vice, although I do as I'm told because she scares the life out of me. I follow her out of the room and along the corridor to a private side room.

She continues in the same hostile voice, "Go into the bathroom and take off your things. I'll get you something to wear."

I do as I'm told, and drop my blood-and-vomit-soaked tunic to the floor. Even my bra has blood on it, so I take it off, followed by my shoes and trousers. The smell of them makes me heave, so I kick them to the side. My knickers, at least, are okay, so I leave them on. I reach for the towel that hangs on the rail, wrapping it around myself, shivering as I wait for Sister to come back.

The door opens, and her voice fills the room. "I've left a bag for your dirty clothes and there's a gown on the bed. Put it on and get into bed."

I hear the door slam as she leaves.

I mimic her as I walk back into the room. "*Put it on and get into bed.* Bossy cow." However, I begin to do as she says, still feeling like a naughty child. I pick up the gown and stare at it in dismay. It's a theatre gown, which means there's no back to it; it just fastens behind with four ties. I shake my head,

---

32

wondering who the hell designed these. Some kinky sod, obviously, a man. Where's the dignity in this? And then I realise I'm wearing my lace thong. Great. Why did I not put my Bridget Jones pants on?

I place my arms through the holes, wrapping the rest of the gown around myself, and pull my hands to the back of my neck as I try to fasten the tie. I manage the first and move down to the next, but I can't quite reach it. I try again, but I'm all fingers and thumbs. I give up on third attempt, not wanting to dislocate my arms. I walk quickly over to the bed, holding onto the gown at the back with one hand and pulling back the sheet with the other. I feel very exposed as I climb in.

The bed's not very comfortable. I try to sit up, moving the pillows up towards the headboard. I shuffle up the bed and nearly strangle myself with the gown. I sit in a daze with my back against the headboard, thinking about all that has happened today.

I jump as the door to my room opens abruptly, swinging back and banging against the wall. A nurse walks in – the same one who came into the staff room earlier this morning – holding a pot with two pills inside and a glass of water. She slams the pot down onto the side table, glaring at me as she does so, then bangs down the glass of water so hard that the liquid spills over the top.

I don't know what to say, so I just stare at her. She obviously doesn't like me, although I have no idea why. She's slim, very pretty, with long blonde hair tied up in a ponytail. I'd guess she's about the same age as me, twenty-six. I notice her name badge on her uniform: *Deputy Sister Darcy*. She's still glaring at me, muttering something under her breath that I don't quite catch. She whips her head around and sniggers, then turns and leaves the room, slamming the door behind her.

I sit in my bed and look at the pills, the spilt water and the slammed door. I really don't know what I've done to deserve this treatment from everyone. What is this place, the Dark

Side? Wow. Everyone is so friendly and kind; I'm going to love working here. Not. I shake my head in amazement, and a pathetic squeak gurgles in my throat.

I take the pills, hoping at least to get some sleep, thinking that perhaps things will look different in the morning. I snuggle down onto the pillow and wince as I try to get my head comfortable, but it's too sore. I let out a deep sigh and close my eyes. As I try to sleep, I hear voices outside my room.

"Yeah, she's in there. Like we've not got enough to do without looking after stupid students. Especially flirty ones. Did you see her around Mr Scott? Stupid bitch."

I feel my stomach turn over as a second voice chimes in.

"He didn't half shout at you, Darcy, wanting you to go and clean up the treatment room after him."

I hear a disgruntled huff from Darcy.

"Tell me about it, Emily … I was fuming when he spoke to me like that."

I cringe as I listen to Emily reply.

"I wonder why he looked after her himself, instead of telling Sister to do it. It's not like Mr Scott to do something like that, is it? Or do you think he fancies her?"

"I don't know," Darcy snaps back. "Do I look like a bloody mind-reader?"

Emily sniggers.

"Are you jealous?"

Darcy shouts this time, and I wonder if they know or care that I can hear them.

"Piss off, Emily."

I hear them both walk away.

What's going on? It seems like I've accidentally started some kind of war. I rub my hands over my face, catching the dressing again.

Ouch!

I want to go home and start this day again. This was supposed to be my fresh start. I close my eyes, feeling suddenly sleepy. The pills are kicking in, I realise. They're

—

very strong, and I start to drift off.

I dream about him.

He's grinning at me with his megawatt smile, whispering lewd things into my ear. I'm shocked by what he's saying; his remarks are forward and suggestive. No, they're more than that – they're downright shameless, brazen even. I'm blushing. He notices, and he seems to like the power he has over me. He moves closer, and he's about to kiss me. My heart starts racing, but I want him to kiss me all the same. Oh dear Lord, what am I thinking? He's arrogant, bossy and intimidating. I certainly don't like him.

The sound of the door opening wakes me from my sleep and I sit up, knowing that my face is flushed. I open my eyes to see Alison, the student nurse who buzzed me in, smiling kindly as she comes into the room. When she speaks her voice is soft.

"Hi. I hope you don't mind – I thought I'd just call in to see how you are."

I return her smile and point to my head. "I'm sore."

"Have you had something for it?"

I nod.

"Good. I was so worried about you when I saw all that blood."

I smile again.

"Do you need anything?"

"No. I'm fine, thank you. Actually, could you do me a favour and ask Sister if she managed to get hold of my husband for me, please?" I'm still worried about what I did this morning, and what his reaction is going to be.

"Of course I will," she answers, nodding her head. "I'll go and ask her for you now."

I smile as she leaves the room, pulling the sheet over me. I'm getting increasingly worried about what Adam will say, and what Alison's going to tell me when she returns. I know that he'll be annoyed.

Alison returns and looks at me with a raised eyebrow.

"I asked her for you, and she said she'd left him a message on his mobile to ring the ward, but he's not called back as yet."

She's looking at me as though she wants to say something else, but she simply smiles.

I know Adam's making me stew by not ringing, playing his mind games again. Any decent person would have rung back straight away, and I know he always has his phone switched on, meetings or no meetings. But he's not a decent person. He wants me to panic and stew, to work myself up wondering how he's going to react. It's all part of his sick game. I raise my head slightly.

"Thank you, anyway."

"No, problem. Is there anything else I can do for you before I go?"

I shake my head.

"I'll call and see you in the morning, if you want me too. I'm on an early shift. Oh, I nearly forgot – I got your bag for you from the staff room."

She hands me my bag. I thank her again as she's leaving the room. I feel drained, and I'm not sure now if it's the pills or the thought of Adam and his mind games. I really don't have the energy or inclination to cope with him any more. I'm worried, but surprisingly not as much as in the past. My eyes feel heavy and I'm struggling to keep them open. Sleep overtakes me once more, and I drift off into a world of darkness.

I wake. I don't know how long I've slept, but it's dark outside. I switch on the side light and take my phone out of my bag, checking the time. It's 10.45 p.m. I've had one text message from Adam, at 8 p.m., and a voice mail from early this morning. I don't bother listening to the message; I know exactly what it will say. The text, though, I read.

I have to work late; an emergency has come up. I'll visit you in the morning if I have the time.

36

I screw my eyes shut and think, here we go, it's the start of some sick little game he wants to play. But I don't want to play his sick mind games any more. Stuff him. I'll ring him before he can ring me. That will shock him; I've never done that before. I was always too scared but, being away from him, I don't feel as afraid any more. I ring his mobile; it goes straight to voice mail so I hang up. I ring his work number and Steven answers.

"Hi, Steven. Can I speak to Adam, please?"

"He's not here. He went home about two hours ago."

"Oh, okay. Thank you."

I hang up before he starts quizzing me on Adam's behalf. I check the text message from Adam, received at 8 p.m. I ring the house phone; it goes to the answer machine. I leave a message, because I know he always checks the messages, no matter what. It's an obsession with him, like his mobile phone. I'm feeling cross as I leave the message, so I snipe at him.

"If you have the time, don't bother coming!"

I shouldn't have said that, but it's done now. I've had enough of him. I hang up. I need my strength now if I've to deal with him in the morning. Well, that's if he can even be bothered to show up, which I hope he doesn't.

I climb out of bed, wobbling a little, making my way to the bathroom by holding on to the wall. I catch sight of myself in the bathroom mirror. I have a huge dressing on my head. I take a closer look, noticing streaks of blood down my face, on my chest and in my hair. And I stink of blood and vomit. No wonder no one wanted to stay in the room and talk to me.

I start to run the shower. I find some toiletries in the cabinet, and there's the large bath towel that I put back on the rail earlier. I untie the tape and the hospital gown falls to the floor. I remove my thong, walk over to the shower and step inside. The water cascades down my body; it's warm and soothing. I reach for the shower gel, squeeze a large amount on my hands, then rub it over my skin – around my neck and over my breasts, down towards my stomach, and then back over my breasts. The gel feels good on my skin, and it smells fresh and clean. I let out a deep sigh. I start to run my hands back down my body, over my stomach again and then my legs, noticing the bruising there and on my hips, bruises that Adam caused.

This time I'm determined. No more.

I close my eyes as I move my hands back up my legs and then across my tummy. My hand lingers there. As I close my eyes, I let out another long breath, saying out loud, "Come on, Abbie, you're sorting it."

Am I? I think. Sorting it how? God, only knows, but I will. I continue to rub the shower gel over my body, washing away the sick and blood. I'm feeling more relaxed, and the memories of the bad day I've had are finally leaving me.

"Bad day," I mutter. "That's an understatement. Bad four years."

I'm suddenly disturbed by a noise, the sound of a door opening. I shout, "Hello?" but no one answers. I shrug it off, thinking that it's probably the plumbing. I carry on showering. I don't wash my hair as my head feels far too sore for that.

When I'm finished I feel a little better, but as I step out of shower I hear the same noise – the door to my room opening or shutting. I wrap the large towel around myself and shout louder this time. "Hello?"

Still no one answers.

I step into my room, but nobody's there. I open the door onto the ward corridor and pop my head out. The dimly lit figure of a man, tall and dark haired, turns the corner at the end of the corridor and approaches the doors that lead off the ward. The main lights to the ward and corridors are switched off, so it's too dark for me to make out who he is. Before I even get the chance to ask, he's disappeared.

I shake my head and return to my room, knowing he probably wasn't visiting me anyway. I put the designer gown back on and place the towel in the bathroom. My thong goes into the carrier bag with my other clothes. Then I climb back into bed. I've just covered myself over with the sheet when there's a light tap at the door. It opens and a nurse enters.

"Hi, Abigail. I'm Samantha. How are you feeling now?" she says, smiling and friendly, which is a novelty around here.

"To tell you the truth, I'm feeling a little better after my shower, although my head is still splitting," I say back, smiling towards her.

"I'll get you something for that. Do you want anything to eat?"

"No, thank you, but a hot drink would be nice, please."

"No problem."

"Oh, sorry, can you tell me, please, has my husband rung?" I cringe inwardly, dreading her answer.

"No, sorry. No one has called for you."

I say nothing, but I'm relieved all the same. She leaves the room to get my drink and tablets, returning in record time.

"Here you go," she says pleasantly, popping two pills into my hand. Then she passes me my coffee.

"Thank you." I put the pills into my mouth and take a sip of the coffee.

"Anything else you need, just ring the nurse-call."

I smile. "Thank you. Oh, can I ask you something else, please?"

She nods.

"Were you in my room before?"

She looks puzzled.

"No. Why?"

"I thought I heard someone, that's all."

"Oh, well, Mr Scott came to your room to see you just before me. He stayed briefly, and then left. Didn't you speak to him?"

"No. It must've been while I was in the shower."

She raises her eyebrows at me, and looks amused. I don't say anything but I know she can see the confusion in my eyes.

She grins and continues in a matter of fact voice. "I think

you've made quite an impression on our sexy surgeon, Abigail."

I nearly choke on my coffee.

"Why do you say that?"

"Really, do I need to spell it out to you?" she remarks, shaking her head at me. "Mr Scott is normally very reserved. He never speaks to anyone on the ward, not staff anyway. He's very professional and insists on silence when he speaks, but today we all saw a different side to him. He seemed rather flustered, and he's usually so calm and controlled. We've never heard him swear, well, not at work anyway, or on the ward before, but he did today. Everyone was talking about it. He shouted at staff, when normally he'd just give Sister a look, and she'd know immediately that he's not happy with something."

I'm looking at her, stunned.

She continues, looking at me in surprise. "You had a nasty bang to your head, and he would never do for anyone else what he did for you today – looking after you like that. You're the talk of the ward." She bends closer to me. "Although, between you and me, I think a few of the nurses are as jealous as hell!" She's nodding her head at me. "His reputation precedes him, treating women like …" She pulls in her lips tight, shaking her head. "Well, let's just put it this way – he doesn't have girlfriends. More like one-night stands, and he's left a very long line of broken hearts behind him, so I'm led to believe." She carries on, painting a very clear picture of this particular bachelor. "He never speaks to us mortal nurses, and no one's ever known him to speak to a student. He's far too important and grand for that, and he's absolutely loaded."

"Really?" I croak.

She continues in a slow whisper, as if she's about to tell me some juicy gossip.

"Yes, really, and visiting a patient who's a student, at this time of night, eleven o'clock." Her voice has changed to a loud pitch, and I wonder if she's laughing at me. She shakes her head. "Oh my God, girl. Wake up and smell the coffee!"

And with that she leaves the room.

I'm so confused by her words. Oh my Lord, he was in my room when I was in the shower; that noise I heard, the door opening. I shake my head and finish my coffee, thinking about what the nurse said. My head is killing me; I feel like I'm wearing a concrete helmet.

I can't keep my eyes open and I'm mumbling his name as I drift off to sleep once again. He wouldn't dare, would he? He's very cocky, that much is certain. I'm so confused by him, and I don't know why he's affected me the way he has. Do I like him? Then blackness.

I'm woken by the sound of Adam's voice. I cringe internally, wondering why he's come to the hospital, but then I remember: he knows I'm changing and the first chance I have I'm going to leave him. He's talking to a nurse outside my room. I can hear her giggling flirtatiously with him, and I know that he's turning on the charm with her, and that he doesn't even care that I'm in the room and can hear his slimy voice.

"Really, you look very pretty in your uniform."

She giggles. Women fall for that so easily, especially from him. I know I did. His good looks, his charm, his flattery, his blue eyes. But not any more. I can see into those blue eyes clearly now; I can finally see the truth – the heartache he's caused me, the misery created by his selfishness and abuse. I stare at the ceiling, knowing that I'll be on the receiving end of his bad temper and nasty tongue, that I'll be punished for the message I left on the answer machine.

He walks into the room wearing a fake smile that I immediately want to bounce off his face, because I know he's only doing it in case there's someone in there with me. He's wearing the same black suit I last saw him in, the same pale-blue shirt and tie. His jacket is over his arm. It's light outside. I look at the clock and see that it's 7.30 a.m. He's unshaven, wearing the same clothes as yesterday, and I know he's not been home. He walks towards the bed.

"Oh, Abbie, what happened to you, babe?"

I look at him, surprised. Babe? What sick game is this?

I stare at him as I ask, "Have you been home? What time did you finish with your emergency at work?"

He's mad, pulling a face at me as he slings his jacket on the bed. When he answers, it sounds defensive and uncaring, as usual.

"Yes, I've been home, and for your information I didn't leave work till 2 a.m. I rang the ward, and I also rang you this morning, which clearly you chose to ignore, along with the voice mail I left."

He's watching my face, checking for my reaction. I muster a smile. I know he's lying, but I don't want him to make a scene, not at work. I just raise my head. He throws me a look, continuing through gritted teeth, warning me not to answer him back or else.

"The nurse said it would be better if I came in the morning. Which I have. Do you have a problem with that, Abigail?"

The warning is clearer now, but I continue to stare at him, reminding myself of what he is, what he's like, and that I can't pretend any more. I can't carry on in silence just to stop the arguments, just so that he won't beat me whenever he feels like it, or because I've disobeyed him. I shake my head at him slowly.

"Really." I say, and I can hear how cynical I sound.

He closes his eyes dismissively. Normally I would have walked out, not wanting a confrontation.

"Can I use the bathroom?" he snaps, and I know he's trying to hold his temper because of where we are.

"Whatever. Help yourself," I reply in the same cynical tone.

He starts muttering under his breath, but loud enough so I can hear him.

"Just fucking wait till I get you home."

42

He turns and heads towards the bathroom, but glances back at me before entering with that look I'm all too familiar with. I can hear him still mumbling to himself, and I know I'll pay dearly for that comment later. But *What happened to you, babe?* He's never said anything like that before. His phone starts to ring. I pull a face, knowing he'll answer it, even in the bathroom. That phone is like a second skin to him. It's never out of arm's reach, glued to him twenty-four seven. He doesn't answer it, although I can hear him shouting.

"Shit!"

Money falls to the floor, as if he's going through his trouser pockets, looking for his phone. I wonder why he's so flustered, why he hasn't answered it, since it keeps ringing. Then I realise it's in his jacket pocket. I put my hand into the pocket and pull it out, but it's stopped ringing. I hear the chain flush, and I notice the caller details. *Nicky.*

I stare at the bathroom door, my expression contemptuous. I hear him pull up the zip on his trousers. I need to find out who Nicky is. I get off the bed with his phone in my hand. I have to leave the room with it because I know that if he sees me with it he'll take it off me. He's done it before when he's caught me going through it. I had my suspicions then that he was fooling around. He got so angry with me that he beat me. I've still got the bruises to show for it, but as usual I gave in and apologised for doubting him. He fed me some crap, and I pretended to believe him just to stop the arguments. I don't feel as timid now, maybe because we're in public.

I leave the room quickly, before he comes out of the bathroom, holding onto the back of my gown with one hand, his phone in my other. I run towards the staff toilets and make my way inside. A few seconds later I hear him shouting.

"Abbie?"

He asks people if they've seen me. I hear someone answer.

"No, sorry."

"Abbie, Abbie!"

He knows I have his phone, and he sounds worried. I scroll through it and find loads of text messages from Nicky. There's also a voice message. I press play, needing to know what it says. I hear a woman's voice; she sounds happy. I pull my lips in tight while I listen to the message. Missed call, Nicky, 7.34 a.m.

"I'm glad you stayed over last night, and didn't go to see h—"

The message continues, but I don't hear the end. I'm livid. I knew he was lying. No bloody wonder he never leaves his phone out of sight. I see red. I'm fuming. I've had my suspicions, but nothing concrete, and no evidence to confirm them, so instead I've dismissed them. How gullible, naive and stupid have I been? Because he knows that if he plays around it's my way out. I can divorce him.

I scream out loud, "Bastard!"

I hear him shout in reply.

"Abbie!"

Words whizz around in my head. I'm seething. He'd never leave, and he's always too clever – the bruises, and the … I sigh because I can't think about that, not now. I need to focus and be strong. The rest can wait for now, but this I can prove. I scream back at him from the toilets.

"Work, my arse. You've been working all right, but not being paid." An affair. Yes, I've got him. My temper's boiling now. After four years of simmering, I'm ready to blow. I want to hurt him, and hurt him badly. I run to the door, wrenching it open. He's standing in the corridor, staring at me with an expression of self-pity on his face. He knows I'm serious this time. I want to slap his face, hard, but I don't. Instead, I launch his phone at him. It misses, hitting the wall behind him and smashing into pieces. I don't notice that behind me a crowd has now gathered. His expression has changed from self-pity to shock. He's amazed by what I've done, that I'm answering him back. For once in my life, I'm not doing what I'm told.

He shouts at me. "What the hell is wrong with you?"

44

His eyes are darting from his phone to me, and I'm furious. He's more bothered about his phone than my health.

I scream at the top of my voice, "Well, maybe Nicky can lend you one of hers." He goes pale. "Yes, I heard the voice mail. You make me sick."

"I can explain—"

I cut him dead. I don't want to hear his crap, or his lies, any more.

"I never want to see you again, and if you die tomorrow then it won't be soon enough."

I carry on like a mad woman, all my pent-up anger and frustration spraying out on him like the wrath of God.

"You lame, cheating, pathetic excuse of a husband. I can't believe you have the audacity to come here after being with her, after what you've done to me." My strength has come from nowhere, as I mock him. "*Oh Abbie, what happened to you, babe?* Like you care about me. You've never cared." I'm shaking with fury.

"Let me explain," he says, holding out his arms towards me, and I hear the manipulation in his voice that has kept me a prisoner for all these years. I will not continue my life like this.

I shake my head, determined to finish it once and for all.

"Just leave." My voice is flat and unfeeling and I sense the overwhelming tension as he just stands there. His glare is silent, but it's a warning, like he's condemning me. But I know there's nothing he can do to me – not here, not on the ward, not in front of everyone. There are too many witnesses.

He closes his eyes as he bites back the anger, which I can almost see radiating from him. Because he has to back down; he has no choice but to walk away. And I know I'm going to pay dearly for what I've just done.

He turns reluctantly, and I watch him cautiously leave through the main doors of the ward.

I breathe in anxiously, knowing that the path I've just chosen to take is a very dangerous one.

Chapter 5

I'm still standing in the middle of the ward, shaking uncontrollably with anger, although this isn't due to sadness that my marriage has just ended in front of everyone on the ward, or the fact that he's been having an affair. I'm glad he's had an affair because I can finally leave and he has no choice. He has to give me a divorce; I've finally got the proof I need – nothing he's done before could be proven.

I start to feel jittery and nervous as adrenalin kicks in, and kick in big time. Tears sting my eyes as panic and fear begin to take hold and the realisation of what I've just done, of the forbidding path I've just chosen to take, surfaces. But I have stood up to him, something I've never been able to do before. My heart suddenly jumps into my throat as I hear voices behind me. I turn my head slowly, cringing at what I'm about to see. Night staff and patients have wandered from their beds, and Mr Scott is there. He's looking over my shoulder at someone behind me, shaking his head at them. Then he looks back at me, and his eyes look puzzled as he moves forward through the small crowd towards me. I scowl at him, throwing my arms up into the air. God, how humiliating. I try to clear my throat to speak, and as I look at everyone I wish I could disappear. No one moves or says anything, and everyone is staring at me in astonishment.

"Sorry, I'm so sorry," I murmur quietly.

One of the nurses points at my gown and motions with her hands, pulling them together. I realise what she means, and my hands fly to my behind. My face is so red that I'm sure I could light the entire ward. I've just made the most embarrassing spectacle of myself, and, to cap it all off, I've done it half-naked, showing my arse to anyone who cared to look.

I feel humiliated, stupid, embarrassed. Mr Scott is shaking his head at me in sympathy. I turn and run to my room, holding the gown shut as best I can at the back. I go inside, slam the door shut and sit on the bed in a daze.

Seconds later, there's a knock at the door. I know who it is – I can sense it – but I can't speak to anyone right now. I need time and space to get my head around what I'm going to do.

"Go away," I holler as he knocks again. "Are you deaf? Go away." My voice is hostile, but it's ignored as the door opens. I don't move. "Go away. Go away," I say, exhausted now, as he ignores my request. "Just go away, please."

"I can't leave you like this, Abigail." His voice is probing, I think, so I don't move my head to look at him.

I say again, but very quietly this time, "Please, just leave me alone." I feel drained and confused, scared, nervous, and I can't think straight. He whispers something, but I don't catch it. I turn to look at him, but he's already turned away and is walking out through the door. I want to ask him to come back, although I don't know where that sudden urge comes from. I sigh heavily, letting him go, knowing that it's for the best. I'm not in the right frame of mind for talking, not the way I feel. I'm in danger of saying entirely the wrong things. I'm mixed up and better off in my own company.

There's another knock. I close my eyes briefly, sighing again. The door opens slightly and Alison pops her head around.

"Hi, Abigail. May I come in?"

"Yes, of course you can."

She looks at me with pity in her eyes, and takes me by surprise when she dashes over to the bed and throws her arms around me.

"I'm so sorry."

Normally I would push her away, not wanting this closeness to someone, preferring to be left alone, as I've always been, but this time I don't. Instead, I rest my head on her shoulder and let out a deep sigh.

"Are you okay? I heard about what happened."

"I really don't know," I reply. "I'm so embarrassed by all

of this. I can't believe I said all those things, and with everyone listening too. I suppose they're all talking about me again."

"Hey, shush, don't do this to yourself. I don't think anyone's talking about you."

"Really? You know what happened, and you weren't even there."

"I do know, yes, but it didn't come from any of the staff on the ward."

"So how do you know?"

She pauses a moment, looking at me, then continues as though she'd been going to say something but changed her mind. She carries on, a little hesitant at first.

"We were in the handover. We heard raised voices and Sister went out to see what was going on. She came back really quickly and carried on with the handover as if nothing had happened. Then Mr Scott came in just as she was finishing and asked to speak to her. They went outside, and she returned a few minutes later saying there'd been an incident on the ward, that it was over with now, and nobody was to ask any questions."

"And did anyone ask anything?"

"No. Well, I think Darcy was going to say something, but Sister gave her a look and she shut up almost immediately. We all know that if Mr Scott's said something to Sister then it's best not to argue. So we don't."

"Does Sister know you're here?"

She pauses again. "Umm, no. I'm meant to be going to the pharmacy for some take-home drugs for you, but I just wanted to see how you were first, as I was passing."

"So I'm being discharged today?"

"Yes, I believe so."

I roll my eyes, saying nothing. I'm nervous about being discharged because I'll have to face Adam. I've nowhere else to go. I can't go to my gran's and burden her with all of this; it will upset her too much. Alison notices how quiet I am and smiles gently at me.

"You're not all right, are you?"

I know she means well, but I feel uncertain of myself. I want to tell her that, no, I'm not okay, but this is the first time I've ever felt like this, the first time I've ever wanted to tell someone about my secret life with Adam. I don't even know her. And while I had the courage to confront Adam today – although where that courage came from, I don't know – the thought of having to go back home to him and carry on with my mundane life as if nothing has happened, until I eventually find the strength to leave, fills me with terror.

Alison pats my leg, her voice soft and sympathetic.

"There, there." The gesture, simple as it is, reminds me so much of my gran that I open my mouth and start to babble.

"I'm a wreck. Look at me! I've nowhere to go. I don't want to see Adam ever again so I can't go home, at least not yet. I need some space to calm down and figure out what I'm going to do, and I can't burden my gran. I don't know what to do, where to go, or who to turn to. I've nobody."

She shakes her head at me.

"You're not a wreck. I honestly don't know what's happened to you, and if you want to tell me then that's fine, but if you don't want to, that's fine too. I can see how much you're hurting. It's obvious that something bad has happened to you, and I don't mean whatever happened between you and Mr Scott. I'd like to help if I can."

My eyes fill with tears. I can't quite believe what she's saying, even though I know she means it sincerely.

She sees my eyes and shakes her head at me, I think before I start to cry. "If you want to – and it's only a suggestion – you can come and stay with me at the nurses' block. I have two bedrooms, so you don't have to go home and face Adam, not yet, not if you don't want to. You can stay at mine until you're ready."

I'm taken aback by her generosity, wondering why she would care so much about a total stranger.

"B-but you don't even know me," I stutter, meeting her gaze. "Or Adam. You don't know what he's truly like."

"No, I don't know you, but I presume a friendship has to start somewhere."

I'm pulling in my lip hard, biting back the tears. I've never really had a close friend before, and certainly not since I met Adam, since he wouldn't allow me to have friends. I had friends at school, like everybody does, but we weren't close. There was nobody I'd confide in, though that had been my own fault – I always felt that people asked too many questions, like they did when I was young.

"Why do you live with your grandparents?"

Or I'd hear people's snide comments: *"Aww, poor little rich girl."*

I never answered, because it hurt too much to think of my parents and how they'd died in a car crash. God only knows, it had taken years for me to forget the nightmare of being trapped in the car with them, of seeing such terrible things when I was only four years old.

I struggle with people, find it so hard to make friends. I'm never sure if their intentions towards me are genuine, or if they're just downright nosey. My gran always says to me that I'm a pessimist, that my cup is always half empty, so I tried for a while to be an optimist, looking at my glass as half full instead, but what has that brought me? Nothing but a very sour taste in my mouth for the past four years.

So I never speak of my parents, or the money I have. I never speak about my private life, and if people find out about it, then they've not heard it from me. The circumstances of my parents' death are common knowledge, as is the wealth they had and the estate I inherited, although the amount of money is just speculation. If someone really wanted to find out then they could easily enough, but I try not to advertise the fact that I'm a Baxter. I keep myself to myself, and muddle through life as best I can.

I smile back at Alison, not really knowing if it's her

---

willingness to help someone in distress, or the thought of her kindness towards me given that we've only just met that makes me want to weep. My voice is croaky from holding back my tears.

"Thank you so much!" And I know by her expression that she can hear the desperation in my voice. "Are you really sure?"

She nods. "Yes, of course I'm sure. It will be nice to have some company."

I smile at her, surprising myself as I lean forward to give her a hug. Apart from my gran, I've not hugged anyone in a long, long time.

"Thank you," I say, and I want to add, *from the bottom of my heart.*

She hugs me back, and then stands to leave.

"Well, that's settled then. Now, do you need some clothes?"

I nod.

"I'll see to it. I'll fetch you something of mine to wear when I'm on my lunch break."

I smile again, ashamed of how badly I misread her yesterday. I'd dismissed her as being giddy and hyperactive, a typical dizzy blonde, but she isn't that at all. She's my saviour, and my first real friend.

"Is this your uniform?" She's looking at my bag, and I nod. "I'll get it cleaned for you if you want me to." She looks at her fob watch and rolls her eyes. "I'd better go before Sister shouts at me for missing the pharmacy slot. I'll see you at lunch time."

I make a cringe-face at her, and she laughs as she leaves.

Once I'm alone, I sit on the bed and feel overwhelmed by her kindness, and the knowledge that I don't have to face Adam. I feel as though a lead weight has finally been lifted off my shoulders.

I get up and go into the bathroom; I use the toilet and wash my hands and face. I really want to clean my teeth but

I've no brush or toothpaste. I mess with my hair, pulling my fingers through it and muttering to myself, "Oh, it needs washing." It's still matted with blood, and I wince with pain as I try to put it in a ponytail. "Ow, ow, ow, that hurts."

Someone knocks at the door.

"Just a minute," I shout, hurrying back into the room and sitting on the bed to cover my exposed behind. There's a second knock, louder this time. I shout. "Come in."

The door opens and my heart jumps when Mr Scott walks in. He frowns at me, his expression stony. I assume he's come to lecture me again for the way I spoke to him earlier, but I don't want to talk about it. And why should I talk to him about it? It's nothing to do with him, so why would he presume that I would? I look at his hard expression again and feel my defences rise, wondering if he expects me to tell him that I'm grateful to him for asking after me. Well, I'm not a pushover like the rest of the women he's been with, just because he's good looking, so I speak immediately, before he has a chance to.

"I said I don't want to talk."

His voice, when he replies, is unfriendly, his manner standoffish.

"I haven't come to talk to you, Abigail. Do you think I make a habit of wandering in to my patients' rooms for a chat?" My cheeks flush, and I see that he notices. "I've come to look at the wound on your head. I am a doctor, or had you forgotten that?"

I don't reply. Instead, I sit silently on the bed. I know my mouth gets me into a lot of trouble at times, but I'm getting increasingly worse at reading both him and the situations that keep bringing us together. His presence in the room makes me feel uneasy, particularly since he doesn't speak either. I know I've annoyed him by snapping at him, but is it any wonder I'm defensive when he's the only reason I'm here? The silence between us stretches uncomfortably, and I begin to wonder if he's waiting for me to apologise.

Just when it seems that one of us will have to say something, the door opens and Sister walks in. She holds a silver tray with dressings on, which she places on the bedside table. I meet her eyes, but she doesn't speak to me either. The situation is becoming increasingly awkward, since I can't make eye contact with Mr Scott when my face is so flushed. The only alternative is to stare at Sister as she unwraps the dressing pack.

Mr Scott glances at her.

"I think I can manage that, Sister," he barks. "Haven't you got other jobs to do?" She scowls at me behind his back, and I know she blames me for his bad mood. She's probably right, I think, but it's still him – Mr Bad Mood – she needs to be glaring at, not me. She drops the dressing pack on the tray and walks out of the room without speaking, closing the door quietly behind her. I glance back at him. I want to tell him not to take his bad moods out on his staff, but the look he gives me is so dismissive that I daren't say anything.

He takes off his jacket in silence, revealing the outline of his chest through the thin material of his shirt. I try not to stare, but I can just make out the contours of his muscles. The material stretches across his powerful shoulders, and I can't help but remember how he picked me up and carried me in those arms with such ease. My stomach flips over as I recollect the memory.

He undoes the dressing pack, removes the gloves and puts them on with nimble fingers. I suddenly feel jittery as he walks towards me. I take a deep breath to calm myself, and as I do I get a waft of his aftershave. It's clean and fresh. His breath catches the side of my face, making me shiver. I close my eyes quickly, trying to dismiss these unwanted thoughts, but it's hard with his face so close to mine. Gently, he places a hand on my cheek and starts slowly removing the dressing from my forehead. His touch is tender, and it makes my pulse race. I keep my eyes closed, not daring to look at him, scared that I might do or say something to embarrass myself since my senses are all over the place.

He removes the dressing, letting his hand linger on my cheek, and I feel my blush deepen. I don't know what to do; he's still in front of me, so very close, his hand still resting on my cheek. He doesn't move, or speak, and I want to open my eyes to see what he's doing, but I feel frozen for what seems like an eternity. My heart starts to beat faster and faster, and I can hear my pulse thudding in my ears. His breath is on my skin and he smells so good. My head is whirling with wicked thoughts, and I need to find a way to stop them. I'm growing hot and flustered, and I silently tell myself off: *Get a grip. Stop this right now. He's so wrong for you.*

Finally, he breaks the silence, his voice commanding, yet gentle.

"Hold this to your head." He takes my hand and places a dressing in it.

I feel goosebumps break out all over my body as his hand touches mine. This is insane, I think. What is he doing to me? He places my hand over the wound, and I feel it starting to shake. I open my eyes to find myself staring straight into his.

"Why's your hand shaking?" he asks softly. He raises an eyebrow and waits for me to answer, but I can't think of anything to say.

I don't know why my hand is shaking. I think it's because he flusters me so much. Or is it the tender way he's just done the dressing on my head, or when he speaks softly to me, or, of course, how he awakens my senses?

When I don't respond, he turns away and takes something off the tray. I want to tell him to leave, that he makes me feel uncomfortable and strange because he's too direct, but I can't find the words. He turns back to me with a clean dressing in his hand.

"You can put your hand down now." He says, nodding.

When I take my hand away, I see that there's blood on the dressing.

He gently places another dressing over the wound,

54

securing it with tape, and breathes out deeply.

"I'll check it again before I discharge you." He removes the gloves and throws them on to the tray, then bends to pick up his jacket. I'm baffled by the situation, and I still don't trust myself to speak. He straightens himself up, putting on his jacket, and clears his throat. "So, it seems you don't want to speak to me, and that's fine. But bear this in mind ..." He bends closer to me, moving to the side of my neck, and whispers confidently into my ear. "I will not ask a second time."

The hairs on the back of my neck stand on end, and a shiver runs down my spine. Without another word, he turns and leaves the room. I don't move, but sit on the bed and gape at the open door, speechless. I hear a bang outside in the corridor, then a clatter, and a woman's flustered voice.

"Sorry, Mr Scott. I didn't see you there."

He makes an impatient noise in his throat and stalks away.

I'm left alone to try to work out what just happened. Did I hear him right? I'm dumbfounded. I feel flustered and irritated, but also aroused at the same time, and I don't know why, especially on top of everything that's happened with Adam. I'm struggling to cope with how I'm feeling.

I try to rationalise what happened a few moments ago. He's a player, and he just played me, I'm damn sure of that. I know it was rude of me to call him a Richard Cranium, and, yes, I did drive through the red lights and almost crash into him, but I think we're even now. It was wrong of him to embarrass me during the handover, and make me faint, but then I suppose I can't put all the blame on him, since Adam was partly responsible for my fainting. I honestly don't know what to make of Mr Scott, but I'm pretty sure he's playing games with me. I feel as though my head is up my arse. I can't seem to think rationally any more, but I smirk knowingly. Well, if it's games he wants, then games he can have. Two can play at that.

I stand up, irritated with myself for letting him do that to me again. Why did I not speak up?

I give a huff of annoyance, muttering out loud, "He's not getting the better of me. Let the games begin."

I jump at the sound of a woman's voice, the same woman who collided with Mr Scott.

"Breakfast, love?"

The housekeeper is standing in the doorway, her trolley loaded with breakfast cereals, toast, tea and coffee. She smiles as she wipes up a spill of milk, and I cautiously smile back at her. "Are you okay?" she asks.

I nod my head, embarrassed that she's caught me talking to myself. She raises an eyebrow at me in amusement. I don't know how long she's been there, or what she's heard, although by the look on her face, I'm guessing she's heard enough.

"I'm Yvonne, the housekeeper. A little word of warning: if you're going to take him on," she gestures with her head in Mr Scott's direction and grins, "then I'd have three Shredded Wheat for your breakfast from now on, if I were you."

"T-take him on?" I stammer. "I don't bloody think so. That's the last thing I want to do."

She rolls her eyes at me, and I know exactly what she's thinking: *Yeah, whatever. That's what they all say.* She smiles as she puts cereal into a bowl and places it onto a tray with two slices of toast.

"Tea or coffee?"

"Coffee, please."

She pushes the trolley into my room, places the tray on the table, and removes the tray Mr Scott left. Then she grins again.

"Enjoy your breakfast."

I look down at the tray. She's put three Shredded Wheat into my dish. I look back at her, bemused, and she winks at me.

"Eat up! You'll need all your strength."

She pushes the trolley out, laughing as she goes, and I'm left to eat my breakfast in peace.

When I'm finished I climb back onto my bed, feeling bewildered and exhausted. I yawn, and my eyes are heavy as I lie down. Alison's words churn over in my head. She said that he'd asked to speak to Sister and taken her out of the handover, and I wonder whether rather than telling her to make sure the staff didn't ask questions he asked Sister to ask Alison to come and talk to me, to see if I was okay, as I wouldn't speak to him. Alison didn't say as much, although she went quiet when I asked how she knew.

I sigh, because if that is what happened, then that was kind of him. I exhale deeply, closing my eyes, thinking, *That man is a minefield.*

A knock at the door wakes me and I open my eyes as Mr Scott walks into my room with a self-confident swagger. I sit up and swing my legs over the side of the bed. I assume he's come to check the wound on my head before he discharges me, but instead he stands so close to me that I have to tilt my head to look up at him when he speaks.

"I've come to talk to you," he says calmly.

I'm not sure what to say, so I watch his face instead. He studies me, his eyes moving away from mine to wander over my body. His blatant appraisal makes me feel vulnerable and exposed, but annoyed at the same time. I'm not sure if he's playing me again.

"I really don't want to talk to you," I reply firmly.

He looks puzzled, but amused.

"I thought you'd say that." He looks into my eyes. "Well then, you can just listen to me."

I nearly choke, taken by surprise at his audacity. He *is* playing me, I'm sure of it.

"I don't think so. And I think it's best if you leave."

"Not until you listen to what I have to say," he replies in an over-confident manner.

I'm struggling to understand what's going on.

"I beg your pardon!" I snap.

He grins.

God, how annoying.

"I don't have to listen to anything you have to say."

He cocks his head to one side, raising an eyebrow at me, and I'm flabbergasted by his arrogance.

"You're right, you don't have to listen. But you will anyway, because I'm not leaving until you hear me out."

I'm a little shocked. I wasn't expecting that. He's so domineering and sure of himself. I've never known anyone like him. He sits beside me suddenly, taking my hand in his, and an electric charge surges through me. I feel hot and nervous. I try to pull my hand away, but he holds it tightly, speaking in a soft tone.

"Abigail!"

Oh, that tone of voice is so soft, captivating.

He pauses a moment, and watches me. "If we're going to be friends, or more than friends, then you need to know something."

His eyes are beckoning me, inviting me, and they hold a hint of amusement too, because he knows exactly what he's just implied. I blink, reminded of what the nurse, Samantha, said to me: *He's a one-night stand man.* I will not be a notch in his bed post, or anyone else's for that matter. I pull my hand away.

"Mr Scott?" I ask, and he raises his eyes confidently. "Do you struggle with numbers?"

"Pardon?" he remarks, puzzled.

I raise my eyebrows at him and reply in an equally puzzled tone, "I'm sorry, but isn't this the second time you've asked me?"

A small smile plays across his face as he recalls his own words. *Bear this in mind … I will not ask a second time.*

"No, Abigail, I don't struggle with numbers, but thank you for your concern."

———

He looks at me, as if to say, *Your turn*.

I'm irritated now, but I won't let it show as I bat straight back at him.

"If I were you, I'd think very long and hard about what you say, and how you reply. Don't forget, I am a woman scorned, so do you really imagine I want to play these silly games of yours?"

He coughs dryly, and I'm amazed by my own boldness. He smiles, which irritates me even more. God, he's infuriating. If he's going to ask me out, then I wish he'd just do it.

"Well," he says, "feisty as well as beautiful! What a fantastic combination."

I'm stunned as he continues, "I need to think long and hard, do I, Abigail, before I reply? Is that what you're saying?"

He rubs his chin, nodding his head at me and smirking for some reason I don't understand. It looks like he's thought of something witty to say, so I wait with bated breath for his response as he grabs my hand again and squeezes it, moving his face slowly towards my ear.

I stay very still, unsure of how to react.

He inhales, and then breathes out softly, sending shivers rippling over my body. He knows exactly what he's doing to me as he whispers my name, rolling it around his tongue like he's tasting it. Just that single word on his lips makes me feel as if I might faint. He smiles at me, and the room lights up. He breathes in again, deeper this time, and I can't catch my own breath for wondering what he's going to say next. When he speaks, his tone has changed, and it brings me out of my daze.

"My name is Edward," he says, matter-of-factly. Then he laughs, and I feel my lips curling in response, my shoulders beginning to tremble. He smiles at me as I shake my head.

"Very funny!"

I nudge him with my shoulder, and he knocks me back gently with his, grinning at me. I'm grinning too, because I really thought he was about to proposition me, though with what I'm not at all sure – a date, a fling? But the way he played out that scene to tell me his name makes me wonder about his sense of humour. After the stunt he pulled in the treatment room, with the towel and his trousers, I'm beginning to get an idea of it now. He makes me smile, and that's a good thing, I'm sure. I don't think a man has made me smile in a long, long time.

He winks at me. "That's nice. You have a wonderful laugh, and a beautiful smile, but your eyes are too sad for my liking. Blue eyes like yours should be smiling." And with that he pats my leg, saying, "I'll wait until you're ready, until you ask for me, until you want me!" He stands and bends over me, gazing into my eyes. He sighs, strokes the side of my face, and walks away. At the door he stops and winks again. "I'll be waiting, Beautiful."

He leaves the room.

Wow! Did that really just happen? He thinks I'm beautiful, he'll wait for me, wait until I'm ready. A shiver runs down my spine, and I get a strange tingling feeling in my stomach. Is he mad to say all that to me? I don't know if I'm flattered or just in shock. I'm shaking my head in disbelief, and I catch sight of myself in the mirror; my hair is a mess – long, thick and uncontrollable. On my forehead is a huge dressing, and a fantastic bruise is forming around my eye. My skin is pale, and my eyes are tired and puffy from lack of sleep.

He thinks I'm beautiful. I think he needs glasses.

"Hmm, Edward," I say under my breath, taking my turn to savour his name, rolling it around my tongue. Now he's quite the demi-god. I bet woman fall at his feet, just as he expects them to, and I'm reminded of Samantha and Yvonne's words of warning. He obviously has a bad reputation. I shouldn't even be thinking like this, and I certainly shouldn't be feeling like this. I should listen to my subconscious instead.

He's a spider and you're a fly, and he thinks you're beautiful. You, Abigail Baxter. He's drawing you in! You're already up his winding stair, and looking into his parlour.

Alison bursts into my room and I nearly fall off the bed in surprise.

"Come on, I've brought you some of my clothes," she announces, and puts them on the bed. "We're about the same size, aren't we? An eight, or maybe a ten? And I think we're about the same height, five six or so."

She laughs as I nod.

"Gosh, if you were a blonde instead of a brunette then we could be twins! Now, get dressed – you're coming home with me. You're all discharged and ready to go. I've got your pills here as well." She shakes the bag and the pill bottle rattles inside.

I pick up the clothes.

"Thank you. I really do appreciate this."

She smiles.

"No need to thank me, honestly. I'm looking forward to you staying!"

I go into the bathroom with the clothes. I dress in a bra that's too tight and makes my breasts look enormous, a T-shirt that's equally tight, and a pair of yoga pants that are a very snug fit around my bottom. I put on the trainers – they're the only things that fit correctly. I look in the mirror, rolling my eyes at myself. Dear me, I look like I'm about to audition for a kinky aerobics class on a late show for Channel 4. I walk out of the bathroom and Alison grins at me.

"I think you're a little bigger than me in the top department."

"Umm, I think you might be right there!"

"Are you okay?" she asks.

I nod my head.

"I've got your bag and pills. Are you ready?"

I nod again.

"Ready!"

I smile gratefully at her as we leave the room. I stop to say thank you to the nurses. We're about to leave the ward when Mr Scott comes out of his office and speaks to Alison.

"Hi, Alison."

She smiles at him, and replies casually, "Hi, Mr Scott."

I watch them, puzzled by the exchange. I'm sure that Samantha said he never speaks to any of the nurse on the ward, especially students. I wonder if Alison knows him.

He nods at me, but doesn't speak. His eyes roam around my body, making my temperature and heart rate rise.

I blush, but he doesn't stop looking. I walk past him, and Alison follows.

He speaks softly to me. "Take care, Abigail."

My response, for some reason, is a squeak, although I really want to giggle, because I think I do quite like him at this moment. Well, when he's not being so arsey, that is.

"Thank you … Edward."

He nods, and my blush deepens. Alison watches us both and laughs.

"Come on, Abigail."

"Umm, sorry," I reply nervously to her as Edward continues to undress me with his eyes.

He's amused, knowing exactly what he's doing and how he affects me. I'm doing it again, getting flustered around him. I shake my head, and start to walk down the corridor, trying my best to ignore him. We stop at the doors, and I turn back to look at him before walking through. He's still openly watching me, and he winks, which, oddly, makes me grin.

He laughs, and I can still hear him as I'm walking through the doors onto the main corridor. And somehow, I don't know why, I think it's nice to hear laughter and, more so, for me to smile. Then I wonder, as I walk down the corridor with Alison, if we'll become friends.

Chapter 6

I'm still smiling to myself as we reach the doors to the main entrance.

"It's this way," Alison says as the door automatically opens and she points for us to turn left.

I pull my arms around myself as the cold wind hits me.

"Gosh, it's chilly," I mutter through chattering teeth.

"Hmm, it is. Sorry, I should have brought you a jacket, but I didn't think. Would you like to borrow my cardigan?"

I shake my head, although I'm touched by the gesture.

"Come on then. If we walk fast I'm sure we'll warm up. It's not that far." She points towards three large red-brick buildings at the far end of the hospital.

We start to pick up speed as we walk along the path towards the nursing accommodation. As we're approaching, Alison points again, like a tour guide, and I can't help but feel pleased that she seems to be looking forward to me staying with her.

The three two-storey buildings stand side by side, with a large car park in front. Trees separate the path from the car park, and the leaves are a beautiful colour as they fall, swirling around on the ground. Alison nods at the building, continuing to point.

"One and two the nurses' blocks; number three is for the doctors." She smiles as she says the last word. "We're in number one, flat five."

We walk through the car park and stop at the double glass doors.

"These are for the rubbish. The green one is for normal waste, and the blue is for glass, bottles, recycling stuff," she says, pointing to the large bins tucked away at the side of the door as she punches a number into the key pad. "You need to remember this: seven, six, five, four." She laughs. "Hard, isn't it?"

I grin back at her.

The doors open into a corridor with five flats on either side. Alison nods towards the mail boxes on the wall. "This is where the post is left. You can have yours delivered to mine if you want." She points to her mail box as we walk past.

"I don't think I'll get any post while I'm here," I comment, "but thank you anyway."

"You never know, you might," she says as we stop outside her flat. She removes her keys from her bag. "Oh, that reminds me – I'll get you a key cut tomorrow." She wiggles the key in the lock and opens the door, gesturing with her hand for me to enter. "Well," she says with a smile, "this is home."

I look at the spacious lounge area with a sofa and two oversized, comfortable-looking chairs. It's larger than I'd expected. An enormous television has been mounted on the wall, and lamps sit on side tables scattered about the room. I see a coffee table and it makes me cringe as I remember my last disastrous run-in with a one during the handover.

The lounge smells newly painted; the walls are all in creams with the exception of one in a deep shade of mulberry that makes the room feel warm and inviting. Alison throws her bag on to the sofa and takes my hand, saying excitedly, "Come on, let me give you a tour! This is the kitchen."

I pop my head in, but before I can take in the room she's pulling me out to continue with the tour.

"The bathroom's through there, and there are two bedrooms."

"It's lovely," I say honestly.

"It's okay."

"Everything looks brand new."

"Yes, my dad had it all re-done for me before I moved in." She sighs. "He's nothing else to spend his money on now, not since my mum left." She suddenly sounds sad.

"Oh," I murmur, not really knowing what else to say.

She shrugs, and we move on to the bedroom.

"This is your room," she says, opening the door. I smile at her, but as I look into the room I feel my face drop. "Are you all right?" she asks, noticing the change in my expression. "Don't you like it?"

I close my eyes for a second, taking a moment to answer her. The colour reminds me of the room at home, the room I never go in. I take a silent breath, not allowing myself to think about that now.

"It's great!" I say remorsefully, opening my eyes. "I'm just a bit overwhelmed, that's all."

"Okay, if you're sure. I'll make us a drink and leave you to settle in. What would you like?"

"I'll have a coffee, please. And thank you for this."

She nods uncertainly.

"I mean it – thank you for everything you're doing for me. It's really kind of you."

"No problem. You take your time, and I'll make us that coffee."

I take a deep breath, trying to compose myself before I enter the room. It's painted a pale yellow. I run my hand down the side of the wall, near to the door. A feeling of emptiness starts to grow inside me and I clench my fists, muttering to myself, "Come on, Abigail. Stay strong." I wander over to the bed and sit for a minute. It's a big room. Two large windows hung with white curtains flood it with light. A double bed with a crisp white duvet cover and pillows sits against one wall. An oak wardrobe and dressing table take up another; and finally there are two chests of drawers and bedside cabinets. That's a lot of furniture for my pills and uniform, I think, because that's all I've got with me. I wonder how I ended up here – a guest in someone's spare room – at this point in my life.

Alison shouts from the lounge, making me jump a little.

"Abigail, your coffee's ready!"

"I'm coming."

I make my way to the lounge and she passes me my coffee. As we sit and sip our drinks, Alison tells me more about herself. She describes her mum and dad, and how her dad spoils her now that they're divorced. She tells me where she went to school, and all about her past boyfriends. She's sweet and kind, and her stories seem to calm me.

Later we watch a musical on the telly. Alison makes me laugh as she sings along to the songs and tries to get me to join in. As the afternoon wears on we cook a simple meal, one of my gran's quick, healthy pasta dishes, with chicken and garlic mushrooms. We sit at the table eating, and I think about how grateful I am that Alison is making this so easy for me.

"Gosh, you're a very good cook." She smiles as she tucks in.

"Thank you."

"Where did you learn to cook like that?" she asks, sitting back in her chair and rubbing her stomach. "It was so quick and delicious, and I can't believe it was low fat!"

"My gran taught me," I reply, smiling as I start to clear the plates. Alison shakes her head at me.

"No, let me do that. You cooked!"

"It's fine, honestly. I'd rather keep busy. Besides, you helped." I do want to keep busy, because I know if I stop that I'll start thinking of Adam, and what he's going to do now he's realised that I'm not going back. "Please let me do this," I add, "to say thanks."

She relents. "Okay."

I pick up the dishes. "Why don't you go and have a bath? I'm fine here. And, Alison, please call me Abbie."

"Okay, Abbie. I'll grab that bath" – she smiles – "and then I'm going to ring Tom."

"Tom?" I asked puzzled, because she's not yet mentioned a Tom to me.

"He's my boyfriend," she says with a giggle. "He's a doctor in A and E. I met him not long after I started. He's friends with Edward. I mean, Mr Scott."

"So you know Edward?" I say, then I suddenly wonder why I'm asking that question.

"Yes, although not very well. He's been here a couple of times to pick Tom up. And I've seen him at Tom's a couple of times; he's got a flat in the doctors' block, because he works on call and has to do nights occasionally. Edward usually stops over at Tom's when they go out of town for medical functions, stag parties – you know the type of thing." She rolls her eyes. "Lads' nights out. Although nine times out of ten Tom stays here because Edward takes back his – "

She stops abruptly, and looks at me.

"Takes back his what?"

"Nothing. Forget I mentioned it. I shouldn't have said anything."

I don't pry, and it's easy enough to guess what she meant. He takes back his one-night stands and, of course, what he does is nothing to do with me. I still can't help wondering why I'm asking these questions.

"Anyway," Alison continues, "I'll go and get that bath – if you're sure you don't mind."

"No, you go ahead. I'll just clear away in here and then I think I'll ring my gran."

Once I've finished in the kitchen I go to my room and retrieve my phone from my bag. I've a few messages and missed calls from a private number. I look at my screen, puzzled, and then roll my eyes. They must be from Adam. I look at the text message first. 9.30 a.m.

You'll regret doing this, believe me.

Nothing else, just that. I press to hear the voice message.

"You'd better come home today, Abigail. Discharge yourself and get home, if you know what's fucking good for you."

They're all the same – more threats that I'd better go home, or else.

The last one is the most disturbing, sent today at 15.25 p.m.

———

"I'm warning you now – if I have to ring you or text you again because you haven't come home, I'll come and fucking find you. You think I've been a bastard before, but it's nothing compared to what I'll do to you if you're not home today. Got it?"

His voice is nasty; I can hear the loathing. My hands are shaking at the thought of him, but I remind myself that he doesn't know where I am. Nobody does. Even if I tell my gran where I'm staying, he'll not go to her house. I know these are just empty threats and mind games, his way of trying to keep me under control. He won't come to the ward because it's too public. He won't risk anyone seeing what he's really like.

I'm just about to delete the messages when I hesitate; something tells me to save them.

I scroll through my numbers and stop at my gran's. My finger hovers over the call button, but then I think better of it, for now at least. I'll ring her tomorrow. She doesn't know any different yet, since I usually ring her on a Wednesday before we meet, and I don't want to worry her before I have to. I've a full weekend with her to look forward to this week, and the thought of it makes me smile.

I place my phone on silent and walk back into the lounge, where I meet Alison coming from her room. She's wearing her pyjamas, and carrying a pair for me. She hands them to me.

"I hope these are all right for you."

"Thanks," I say, taking them.

She yawns, and though I try not to, I immediately follow suit. We laugh, and apologise at the same time.

"I think an early night's in order, don't you?" she says.

I nod, relieved she's mentioned it first, because once again I'm shattered. I think it must be the pills they've given me.

"Night. I hope you sleep well," she says,

"You too, Alison," I reply with an uncertain smile, wondering if I will sleep.

I decide not to tell her about the messages from Adam.

I make my way to my room, undress, and put the pyjamas

on. The top's a little tight around my breasts, but it will do for now, until I can get some things from home. I pull back the duvet and climb into bed. It's comfortable and warm. The pillows are soft, and as I pull the duvet over me I feel safe for the first time in a long while. My head hits the pillow, and surprisingly, after all that's happened recently, I fall asleep immediately.

I wake the next morning to the sound of Alison singing loudly.

"Morning," she says when I walk into the lounge. "Sleep well?"

"Yes, thanks. I think it's those pills; they're very strong."

She looks at me in her pyjamas and tries not to laugh at the tight top.

"Do you want me to drive you home tonight, to pick up some things?"

I look down at the top.

"Would you mind? I can't keep wearing your clothes, although it needs to be before six thirty, if that's okay with you."

She nods and doesn't ask why, guessing that I want to be gone before Adam gets home so I don't have to face him.

"Okay, that's a date. I'll come and get you after my shift, around four."

And with that she's out the door. What am I going to do all day? I've been told by Sister to take the rest of the week off. I start to tidy the lounge, then the kitchen and bathroom. I make my bed, then a coffee, and switch on the TV. "Daytime telly," I mutter, rolling my eyes with a sigh, but I sit on the sofa anyway and watch a chat-show host shouting at his guests. He looks like he's about to burst a blood vessel. I grin at the thought, wishing he would because he's giving me a headache.

My thoughts drift back to what happened on the ward yesterday. I shrug my shoulders, realising that my life is

———

turning into one of these episodes.

I flick through the channels, but there's nothings on.

I take a bath and then dress in yesterday's Channel 4 aerobics outfit. This makes me think of Edward, and I smile. I walk into the kitchen, rummage through the fridge and find some ham; there's brown bread in the bread bin. I make a sandwich and pick at it while I'm sitting on the sofa. I'm not that hungry, and I only eat half of it.

My thoughts keep flicking between going home tonight and Edward. I'm confused; I don't know why I keep thinking of Edward when I know he's wrong for me. He's a one-night stand guy, and that was confirmed by Alison last night, although she didn't say so in so many words. But she didn't have to; it was easy to read between the lines and fill in the missing words. Her reluctance to carry on confirmed that to me, and that's something I'm defiantly not interested in – a fling, or a touch-up behind the bike sheds, so to speak. I roll my eyes at myself, because Edward's words keep coming back to me all the same.

I feel sleepy as the day wears on. I yawn as a film starts on the telly, a romantic comedy. I roll my eyes again, but leave it on anyway because the music's nice and it's better than the chat shows. I yawn again, feeling so tired that I can barely think straight. With the film on in the background, I curl my feet up on the sofa and pull a cushion towards me and hug it. I'm soon fast asleep.

Edward's here, swaggering towards me and murmuring in that chocolate voice of his.

"Oh, baby, you're wearing my favourite top." He winks, coming closer as I hitch myself back on the sofa.

He's so self-assured, but I've pushed myself too far back and I fall over the side. I hit the floor on my bottom, my legs splayed open. I shake my head and roll backwards to land on my knees. He raises an eyebrow suggestively and offers his hand. I find myself taking it, even though I'm not sure if I want to. He grins, dragging me off the floor to my feet and pulling me in tight towards him. I think briefly that I shouldn't be letting him do this, but secretly I want him to. He's holding me tightly. He's strong, and I feel safe.

I shake my head and try to compose myself, knowing that he's luring me in like a spider with a fly. I should pull away from him, but he clicks his fingers and a CD comes on, pushing the thought away. He holds me tight, moving his hips in time to the music, singing the words into my ear. He's drawing me in and I can't pull away.

I start to pant as he seductively sings the words into my ear. "Come on … Come on!"

I feel my head spinning as he lifts my chin. I'm unable to control my senses. His hips roll against me, and I feel him press into me. I blush, knowing what he's doing but unable to stop him. His face grazes mine, his breath on my skin making it prickle with goosebumps. He whispers sensuously, moving his hand to my bottom, lifting me upwards onto my toes.

When he speaks, his voice is a growl.

"Oh … fuck, Abigail!"

I'm shocked at the profanity, but still I don't stop him.

"Oh!" I squeak nervously as he moves his hips back and forth against me, squeezing my bottom hard. I squeal, and it clearly excites him.

"Ummm," he murmurs, the sound a caress against my skin, leaving me breathless with desire. His hand cups the back of my head, his fingers twining through my hair. "Oh, baby," he groans, pulling my hair and twisting it tightly around the palm of his hand, forcing my head back. He moans, long and hard, moving his lips towards mine.

I cry out with excitement.

"Yes!"

His face moves closer. The song continues to play – "Love Me, Baby" – and his lips are almost touching mine. I close my eyes, ready for him, ready to take his mouth and the full force of his lips against mine, when I hear a voice shouting.

71

"Abigail!"

My eyes fly open, and I sit up with a gasp, seeing Alison standing in the doorway, staring at me.

"Are you okay?" she asks. "You were making some very strange noises."

I cringe inwardly.

"Y-yes, I'm fine," I stammer, seeing her raised eyebrows. "It was just a strange dream, that's all."

She tilts her head to one side, looking amused.

"Oh!" she says, with a smirk on her face.

I pray that she doesn't ask me what my dream was about, because I'd not be able to answer her truthfully. I don't know what's going on inside my own head just lately, and I can't explain the feelings that I seem to be developing for Edward.

There are memories, too, that I've tried to bury deep inside, and that came back yesterday when I saw my room.

And there's Adam. There's always Adam. He's like a bad penny, a rotten apple that's always lurking in the shadows and staring back at me from the bottom of my half-empty glass. I close my eyes, wishing I could turn back the clock, but there's no such thing as time travel. I have to live in this world, the real world, and I'm starting to feel panicky and uncertain again. Alison grasps my shoulder gently, smiling at me.

"Are you ready, Abbie?"

I nod slowly, knowing what I have to do, and that I'm finally about to break the chains that have bound me to him for the past four years – chains of misery, heartache, and, finally, contempt. It's only just beginning to sink in; I am actually doing this, after all these years.

I take a deep breath, hold it in, and then release it. I need to start my life again, a life free of him. I have to stop letting Adam get into my head with his vicious mind games. Alison squeezes my shoulder again, realising that I'm scared.

"Yes, I'm ready," I reply.

———

"Are you nervous?"

I nod. "Yes, a little."

I ought to be shouting from the rooftops, because this is what I've wanted for years now. But I'm nervous all the same. I'm afraid of the unknown, and scared of what Adam will do and say. Nobody knows him, what he's really like. I'm beginning to have a bad feeling about it all. I think about the message he left, the hate in his voice, and I start to shake. Alison takes my hand.

"It'll soon be over, hon." Her voice is kind.

I know she's right. I need to get this over with, but right now I also want to run and hide. But I can't keep running, or hide any longer. So I grab my keys, put on a brave face, apply my false smile and walk out with Alison to the car.

We climb into her Mercedes Sports. She smiles, rolling her eyes.

"Yes, another one of Dad's presents. I told you he spoils me!"

We set off for my house but I don't have much to say on the way. My mind is whirling, and I can't seem to concentrate. I know Alison's talking to me, but I don't really register what she's saying. I nod occasionally, but I only speak to give directions, and I'm lucky she isn't offended. My stomach is churning as we approach my house. I'm suddenly terrified that Adam will have left work early. We pull up outside and I breathe a sigh of relief when I see his car isn't there. My heart's thudding as I put the key into the lock, open the door and step into the hallway. It's dark, cold and empty.

"Would you mind waiting in here?" I say as I switch on the lights. "I'll not be long."

She wanders into the lounge, replying, "No, that's fine. I'll sit here and wait for you. Take as long as you need."

I glance at the clock: it's 4.30 p.m. I leave Alison in the lounge and make my way upstairs. I've only been gone a few days, but it seems like a lifetime ago that I stood at the top of the stairs, late for work. I hurry to my room and grab a holdall

—

73

from the top of the wardrobe. My hands are shaking as I throw in clothes, shoes, toiletries and makeup. I see the photo of my gran and grandad, with Mum and Dad beside them, on my bedside cabinet. My wedding ring sits next to it. I shake my head.

"Come on, you can do this."

I've not worn the ring for months. I told Adam it was too big. Reaching out, I place the photo into my bag, but I leave the ring. I don't want it, and I don't want him.

I leave my room and make my way down the hall towards the bathroom, but I stop suddenly when I catch sight of the back bedroom. The door is ajar. My heart skips a beat, and I'm flooded with memories. That door is never open. I keep it closed because I can't bear to look at it; it hurts too much.

Don't, I tell myself. *Don't go in. Just go back downstairs and leave.*

But it's too late. I catch a glimpse of the room and it draws me in. I stand at the door, shaking my head with my hand to my mouth. I push the door open and let out a cry as I look upon the half-painted room in pale yellow. I know I shouldn't go in, but I can't stop myself.

I walk slowly inside, stroking the wall gently with the palm of my hand, remembering how happy I was. I started the nursery as soon as I found out I was pregnant. I smiled all the time, feeling an overwhelming love for this little bundle that was growing inside of me, because it was mine, for me to love. I would rub my hand over my belly, talking to my baby all the time, telling it that it was my little ball of happiness and about all the things we would do together; desperately hoping it could hear me, and would know how much I loved it. But those feelings, and the happiness I felt, didn't last for long. Adam made sure of that.

Acid tears sting my eyes, making them burn before the pain hits my heart.

My hands go towards my belly, even though there's nothing there now, just a feeling of emptiness. I stare at the

—

74

half-built cot lying against the wall, the bunny mobile hanging from the ceiling. I screw my eyes shut, but it doesn't stop the tears as they stream down my face.

I hold my hand over my tummy, crying, and whisper to my baby, "I'm sorry. Mummy is so sorry that she lost you, that she couldn't save you, that she wasn't strong enough."

It's still raw even after three months. I stopped coming to the nursery, closing the door and hoping that it would block the memories at the same time. It didn't work. So I built a wall high around myself, trying to be strong, ignoring my own pain. But that isn't really me, not when I think of my babies. I was just fooling myself, and doing a pretty poor job of it.

I notice the toy chest, and the knitted rabbit sitting on top of it. Gran made that for the baby. I so desperately wanted to find it when I came home from the hospital that night, and to hold it close to me, but I couldn't. I couldn't let Adam know what it meant to me, because he'd have taken it and thrown it away as soon as he got drunk, just to be hurtful. So I left it in the nursery with my memories. I pick it up, hold it close to me and breathe in the scent of it. My lip starts to quiver as tears come hard and fast.

"Mine, mine. Why? Why?" I whimper.

I say it over and over again, and it's too much for me. I fall to my knees, consumed by emptiness and a sense of how worthless I feel. I sob, holding the knitted rabbit to my heart, rocking back and forth. I don't even hear Alison as she runs up the stairs and flies into the room. She takes in the scene, seeing me clutching the rabbit on the floor, rocking and whimpering like a wounded animal.

"Oh, Abbie, I'm so sorry!"

She kneels and puts her arms around me, holding me tight. I'm cocooned in my own sorrow, and I can't stop the words from pouring out.

"Why did this have to happen? Why is life so cruel? My beautiful babies, snatched away so young, at twelve weeks and fifteen. It did nothing wrong. I'm not a bad person,

---

honestly. I'm so desperate to hold my babies, to cuddle them. I want it so badly. I need it! I feel so empty inside. The wanting, the yearning, it never fades, never leaves. It just eats away at you. I'm dying inside, and nobody knows or cares. I have nowhere to go, no grave, nowhere to grieve for my sweet angels. Life is so cruel! And he doesn't even care! He should be made to pay for what he's done."

"Who?" Alison asks quietly. "What who's done? Do you mean Adam? Did he do something to you or your baby?"

I stare at her now, not wanting to carry on, knowing I can't relive that night again. She climbs to her feet and holds out her hand for me, her face grim. She helps me up. My legs are wobbling and she puts her arm around my waist to steady me.

"Come on, have we to leave," she says softly.

I nod, still clutching the knitted rabbit. I try to stop crying and shaking. I wipe my eyes with the back of my hand and take a deep breath to calm myself down.

"I'm sorry," I begin. "I shouldn't have said all that. I don't know what's wrong with me."

We leave the nursery, and I close the door.

"It's okay, honestly," Alison says softly. She looks at me; I see a tear in her eye, and I realise she cares. She takes my hand, picks up my bag, and smiles sadly at me. "Come on, let's get you back."

I nod, knowing that I have to leave.

We make our way to the top of the stairs, and suddenly I hear the front door open. My heart jumps into my mouth, and I throw Alison a horrified look, realising with dread that it's Wednesday. Adam finishes work early on a Wednesday and comes straight home to change before going out. That's why I see my gran every Wednesday. I haven't seen her today; that's why it slipped my mind. How could I have been so stupid?

I see him walking through the door. He shouts up to me, his voice a snarl because he hasn't realised that I'm not alone.

"Abbie, is that you? Because if it is, you're a few fucking

76

days late."

Alison's face drops when she hears him. She squeezes my hand tight and whispers to me, "Come on, I'm here. Let's just leave."

I'm getting palpitations. I don't want to face him, don't want to see him ever again, but right now I have no choice if I want to leave. And I do desperately want to leave. He looks up and sees Alison on the stairs, with me hovering behind her. He notices the bag she's carrying, and the knitted rabbit I'm clutching in my hand. His expression darkens as he shakes his head.

"I don't think so," he sneers, and I can't find the words to reply. I just want to leave.

Alison walks past him, saying nothing, but looking him stonily in the eye.

I try to follow her out, my eyes downcast to avoid looking at him, but he throws his arm across the doorway and blocks it, stopping me from leaving. I cringe and close my eyes, waiting for the slap, but it doesn't come.

"Please, Abbie. I'm sorry," Adam wheedles, his voice manipulative. "I'll change, I promise."

For a second, I'm too surprised to speak. I shrug my shoulders, hardly able to believe what I'm hearing. I feel angry, and a little insulted that he'd actually think I might believe his promise to change.

When I speak my voice is calm.

"You'll change? You're not capable of changing. You're sick! Or are you just sorry you got caught? I lost my babies because of you!"

He steps back, shocked, since I've never had the courage to say any of this to him before. I gesture towards the house. "This is all you're interested in, all you've ever been interested in, and now you're scared that all of it will go!"

He looks dismayed to hear me answer him back, and even more so as he begins to realise that I mean what I'm saying.

"Abbie, stop it!" He moves to grab me but I pull away,

---

scared of him. He sees my fear and continues, his voice guarded, "We can work things out. Tell your friend to go and then we can talk, just me and you, like it used to be."

I roll my eyes at him, surprised not only by the words, but that he actually seems to mean them. He's deranged. After everything he's done to me. He must think I'm so weak and stupid. He smiles for all the world as if nothing bad has ever happened between us, but when I look into his eyes all I see is his cold, black soul.

I shake my head. "No!"

And somehow I manage to remain calm, because I know this is just another game he's playing. A cruel, vicious game.

Before he can reply, we're both distracted by the sound of shouting outside.

"Let me past, you silly bitch!"

Adam's face drops, and I hear Alison calling to me.

"I'm sorry, Abbie! I couldn't stop her."

A woman bounds into the hallway as if she owns the place. Her blonde hair flies around and her expression, when she sees me, is scornful. Adam says nothing, and she looks nervously at him. Her eyes flick back to me and she starts to unbutton the red jacket she's wearing. Adam watches her, horrified. I shake my head, and start moving forward towards the door, wanting no part of whatever it is she's doing, but she's blocking the door, her mouth twisted in a cruel smile.

"Well, have you told her yet?"

Adam's eyes are wide, and his face has gone pale. Maybe it's just sinking in with him; he's been having an affair and now he'll have to face the consequences of his actions. I'm damned sure he's not upset because of losing me. He never gave a damn about me, or anyone else for that matter. What he is bothered about is losing the good life he's enjoyed – the money, the holidays, the new cars. That's all going to change now, and he knows it.

He snarls at the woman. "Shut up!" he snaps.

Her eyes hardness in them, fly to mine. Then she starts to

78

grin at me as her hand continues to slowly unbutton her jacket.

Adam shouts again, warning her this time. "I said no! Nicky—"

He grabs her wrist, and she smirks at me, then sniggers. But it's too late. Her jacket falls open and I can see her rounded stomach. She's pregnant, about six months. She starts rubbing her hand over her belly, grinning at me, moving her other hand towards Adam's, placing it on her stomach. He pulls it away, throwing her a filthy look, and I know that look all too well.

For just a brief moment I'm frozen, speechless, trying to comprehend what's going on, wondering, is this really happening to me now? But then I'm angry, so angry, and without thinking I slap him hard across his face. He doesn't retaliate or flinch, just stares at me.

"Abbie, I'm sorry! Let me explain."

I can hear the insensitivity in his voice, and I can't even bring myself to look at him as he tries to justify himself. I don't see how he can, because he knows what he's done, what he did to me while I was pregnant, but he wants me to keep my mouth shut now, not say anything in front of her.

I stare at her now, because she's laughing at me, and it's too much. My temper boils over. I'm seething at them both, but especially her for laughing at me.

"If you weren't—" I shout, but then I stop, unable to finish my sentence. I want to say it, but I can't, because she's pregnant.

She screeches back at me, "What? You'd do what? This?"

She slaps me hard across my face, leaving a stinging mark.

Hearing all the shouting, Alison runs into the hallway just in time to see the woman's hand meet my face. Her eyes dart to mine, and her voice is horrified.

"Abbie!"

Her eyes flash at Nicky. "Don't you touch her again, you hard-faced bitch!"

I just want to leave, but Adam starts screaming at Nicky. "You stupid bitch!"

She looks suddenly scared of him, and her voice is pleading. "Adam, please. I was just defending you. She slapped you first."

Adam glares at her, but then holds his arms up in a grudging apology towards me.

"Oh, please, Adam," she continues. "Let her go. Think of our baby."

I throw my hand to my mouth, unable to comprehend all the bullshit that's flying around. I feel tears stinging my eyes, but I refuse to cry in front of them. All I can hear are those words: *Think of our baby.* I think I'm going to be sick.

"Shut your fucking mouth, Nicky!" he snaps at her.

Nicky looks stunned, and I glare at Adam, shaking my head. I can't believe this is happening to me. She's pregnant with Adam's baby and I lost mine because of him. Why me? It hurts, really hurts. Why is he allowing her to keep her baby when he …?

I shut my eyes, trying to force the memory to the back of my mind, and my heart breaks all over again. My babies died, and I feel as though Adam and Nicky are rubbing salt in the wound. This is killing me.

Alison grabs my hand hard, pulling me through the door. Then she turns and snaps at them both, "You stay away from her!"

She puts her arm around me, guiding me back to her car. I'm in a daze. I feel numb and can't speak. She tries to comfort me as she drives, telling me that everything will be okay, but I don't think it will be.

I sob, unable to answer her, clutching my baby's knitted rabbit to my heart all the way back to Alison's flat.

Chapter 7

We arrive back at the flat and I go straight to my room. I lie on the bed and curl myself into a ball for protection. I rock back and forth, sobbing and holding the knitted rabbit close to me, feeling lonely, worthless and desperately empty inside. I need all this to end. I can't take any more; I'm exhausted, mentally and physically. I've tried so hard to get back on track, to rebuild my life, but I feel like I'm slipping backwards. I need this pain to stop, but I can't stop tormenting myself.

She's pregnant.

Adam couldn't have wounded me more if he'd stuck the knife in and twisted it himself.

My eyes close and I drift in and out of a fitful sleep.

Alison comes in and asks if I'm okay, but I don't answer her. I don't know what to say any more. I feel like my life is a raffle and I always get the losing ticket.

The next thing I know, Tom is here, and I can hear Alison talking to him in the lounge. I can make out snatches of the conversation as she tells him what happened with Adam and Nicky, about her being pregnant, and me losing my babies.

"Is she going to be okay?" he asks.

"I'm not sure. She won't speak to me. She's really upset. I'm worried about her."

"You don't think she'll do anything stupid, do you?"

"I don't know. But I do think her husband had something to do with her losing her babies."

"Really?"

"Yes, poor thing."

I'm past caring now. I'm in such a lonely, dark place and I can't see any way of returning. All the feelings I've tried to hide away these past months are now fresh in my head again, eating away at me and making me feel worthless and empty inside.

"Do you want me to talk to her?"

"No, you'd better not. She doesn't know you, and she froze when she'd realised what she'd said. I honestly think she's terrified of him. He must have done something really nasty to her."

"Do you want me to ask Edward to talk to her? He's asked me about her, and he knows she's staying here with you."

"Really? I thought he didn't do compassion or empathy, especially when it involves women."

Tom laughs lightly.

"Me too, but I have to say, I've not heard Edward talk about any woman before. I think she's gotten to him in a big way, and we all know his reputation: shag them, then leave them!"

"Tom!" she scolds.

"Sorry. I know he's my mate, but it's true."

"I know it is, but you didn't have to be quite so blunt about it. Abbie might hear you!"

Abbie has heard him and, no, she doesn't want Edward to come round and have a word with her. That's the last thing I want. I hardly know him, and this is too personal. It's private – this is my life and I don't want everyone knowing about it.

I get up off the bed before they decide to ring Edward, not that I think he'd come anyway, but I wonder what Tom meant by *She's gotten to him*? I walk into the lounge and catch them by surprise.

"Hi," I say.

Alison opens her mouth to speak, but I stop her. "I heard, and there's no need to explain. It's fine. Please don't ask Edward to come round."

Tom pulls a face at me as Alison digs him in the ribs.

"Tom, I warned you. Sorry about that, Abbie." She rolls her eyes at Tom. "Are you okay?"

"I will be," I say with a weak smile. "May I use the bathroom, please?"

"Of course. There's no need to ask."

I walk to the bathroom and lock the door. I want to scream, No, I'm not okay! I'm not fine! I desperately want to get these thoughts out of my head before they start eating away at me again, but I don't even know where to start. I wish I could collect every sad memory from my mind, put it into a pile and empty it into the bin. But it's not that easy, however much I wish it was.

I go to the sink and run the cold water. I splash it over my face and try to compose myself. I leave the bathroom and go back into the lounge, stopping just long enough to convince Alison that I'm not about to have a breakdown before I head back to my room.

I sit on the bed and pick up my phone. I have a few missed calls from a private number again. I shake my head and don't even attempt to listen to them. I can't deal with them right now. I want my gran. I need her to tell me what to do, what to think, and that everything is going to be okay. I scroll through my contacts to Gran's number, but then I put the phone down. I can't do it. I hesitate and then pick it up again, my hand shaking. I'm a mess, but I desperately need to hear her voice. I call her; she answers and the sound of her voice brings tears to my eyes.

"Abbie, love, are you okay? I've just been thinking about you."

A lump comes to my throat and I don't know what to say to her now.

"Sweetheart, what on earth's the matter?"

I'm silent.

"Darling girl, talk to me. What's wrong?"

"Oh, Gran, it's so good to hear your voice."

"What's wrong?"

I don't want to tell her, but I can't stop myself. The floodgates have opened, and I can't close them.

"Gran."

"Yes, love, I'm still here."

"I've left Adam, Gran."

"What's he done? Has he hurt you?" I can tell from her voice that she's guessed. She might be old but she's not stupid, although I've never told her what he was like. I tried my best to hide that part of my life from her.

"No, he's not hurt me." I hate lying to her, but I can't tell her the truth either.

"Okay." Her voice is questioning. "Are you going to tell me what he's done then?"

I sigh.

"He's had an affair … is still having an affair, and … she's —" I stop. I don't think I can bring myself to tell her the rest.

"She's what?"

I decide not to tell her, not yet. I don't want to talk about Nicky being pregnant; it's too hard for me to digest right now. It's tearing the heart from me again. I'm not a cruel person, but I wish them both the worst of misery, misery that I've had to endure, and now I feel horrible that I'm thinking like this, because it's not a very nice feeling and I don't like myself very much for it.

I shut my eyes, take a deep breath and reply, "Sorry. I'll tell you when I see you. I don't want to say on the phone."

"Okay, so you've left him then?"

"Yes, and I'm staying here at the hospital with a friend."

"You don't want to come here and stay with me?"

I don't want her to worry any more than necessary, and I definitely don't want Adam turning up at her house, which he will do, especially now, if he knows I'm there.

"You don't mind, do you?"

"No, not at all. As long as you're safe. I'm presuming he doesn't know where you are."

"No."

"Good, then he can't manipulate you into going back to him."

"No, he can't. I'm never going back to him."

84

She's silent, knowing there's more, but I don't want to tell her yet. I feel guilty though, and she can hear it in my voice.

"I'm glad about that … that you're never going back to him. You can tell me the rest in your own time. You just concentrate on yourself for a change. I know things have been bad from the start with Adam, and I'm sorry now that I never said anything, but I'm just going to ask you one question, that's all. Has he ever hurt you?"

I put my hand to my mouth, screwing my face up as I lie to the one person I love most in the world, because I simply can't tell her truth. I know it would kill her.

"No, he's never hurt me," I say, and the words nearly choke me.

"Really?"

I can hear the doubt in her voice. She doesn't believe me. I need to hang up before she starts asking me more questions, questions that I'm not capable of answering right now.

"I need to go now, Gran. I'll ring you tomorrow, if that's okay."

"Yes, that's fine, but promise me before you go that you're really okay."

My eyes sting with tears again, because I'm not okay at all. I want to tell her what a monster Adam is, and how much I'm hurting inside. I want a hug from her, to have her kiss my head to make everything better, like she did when I was a little girl.

"Yes, I promise."

We say our goodbyes and I climb back into bed, resting my head on the pillow. My phone bleeps, and a quick check confirms it's Adam. I shake my head, hating him. I put it on silent and place it back on the bedside table. I cuddle my baby's rabbit close to me. This is all I have left; this is my only memory. I start to cry, and find I can't stop.

Eventually my tears dry and I wipe my eyes. I've a bad headache from crying so hard. I sit myself up and place the rabbit on my pillow, stroking it gently, closing my eyes briefly

—

and knowing I have to somehow stop these emotions before it's too late. There's a knock at my bedroom door, then Alison's voice.

"Abbie, can I come in please?"

"Yes."

I muster a smile as she comes in.

"Are you sure you're okay?" she asks.

I nod, not wanting to burden her any more than I already have.

"Tom and I have to go out for a few hours, but if you'd rather I stayed with you then I will. I don't mind."

She's so nice, and she's been so good to me. I shake my head.

"You go. I'm going to take a bath and have an early night."

"Are you sure?"

"Yes, please go. Honestly, I'll be fine."

"Okay, if you're sure."

She leaves the room, but I can hear her talking to Tom in the lounge. "Come on, let's not be long. She's still really upset, although she's pretending not to be."

I shrug my shoulders. I thought I was a better actor than that, but Alison's seen straight through me.

They shout a muffled goodbye and I hear the front door open, then close. I glance at the clock: it's 7.30 p.m. My room is too warm and stuffy, and my head's pounding.

I get up and head towards the kitchen for a glass of water, then return for my painkillers. I take the bottle from my bag and twist the lid, but I can't get it off. I push down hard on it, squeezing it, but it still won't budge. I mutter a curse under my breath.

"Childproof? Bloody adultproof!"

I'm getting really cross with it, and I've very little patience at the moment. I throw it at the wall and the lid flies off. I stare at the scattered pills rolling around on the floor. I gasp as a memory coldly creeps into my mind. It's vivid, as though it was yesterday. I try to shake it away, but the empty bottle and pills strewn across the floor are hypnotising me, reminding me of how close I came to taking them once before, at the time thinking it seemed like my only way out, the only choice I had left. I don't want that memory, not now. I don't want to think of Adam, and why I came so close to taking the pills last time. Why, why did I not see it before it was too late? How did I manage to tangle myself up with him in the first place?

I've a secret about him, about my life with him, one that I've never told anyone, not even my gran. I was always too ashamed of myself, ashamed that I didn't fight back harder, or leave him sooner. Why can't I have that time again – look at him with open eyes and see him for what he really is?

I'd been going through a tough time before I met him. I was lonely; I had no close friends. I suppose I had my gran and Glenda, my gran's housekeeper, and even William, Glenda's husband, but I couldn't talk to them about how I felt, and I know deep down that Glenda would've told my gran, thinking she was doing the right thing. My grandad had died, and my gran was heartbroken, so I didn't feel that I could leave her alone. I decided I wouldn't go to university. I made excuses, telling her that I wasn't sure what I wanted to study, and I felt guilty, after all the years they had sacrificed for me, so this was my time to take care of her.

I found a full-time job as a secretary in a local law firm so that I could stay with her. The easy option would have been to work for her, but I was trying to be independent and stand on my own two feet. Looking back, I'm not really sure why I came to that decision. I only know how much I've come to regret it, because it was there that I met Adam.

He was older than me by six years. He had a promising career for someone so young, and he was ambitious and determined to get what he wanted. He'd already made junior partner in the firm, Holden Brown and Lord, although money meant little to me.

He charmed me, and swept me away with his smooth

talk. He asked me out constantly, paid me compliments, and asked the other secretaries about me. He persuaded them to fill my head with how wonderful and kind he was. I was a little naive. In fact, looking back, I was completely naive.

I never went out, and I'd never dated before. I'd only ever kissed one boy, when I was still at school, and I'd certainly never made out with anyone. I was twenty-one and still a virgin. I'd had plenty of attention and offers from men, but I was never interested in them. I never wanted to become close to anyone. I tried my best to keep myself at a safe distance from any situation where I might get hurt. But Adam pestered the girls I'd become friendly with at work, asking them to take me along to work functions with them, where he would magically then appear, like the ghost at the banquet. He was persistent, asking me out constantly, and he could be so very charming when he wanted to be. He also badgered me all the time about my past, saying he wanted to get to know me better, chipping away little by little over the months until he knew all about my parents, the crash, and, of course, the money.

He changed after he found out more about me, becoming more persistent, ringing me all the time, turning up at my gran's house. He flattered me, tried it on, but I never let him go too far – just a kiss now and then. I wasn't sure of him, and I was confused by my feelings for him. We'd only been dating for a few months when, out of the blue, he asked me to marry him. I was shocked, and deep down I knew I should never have said yes, but I did. God only knows why. I believe now that I accepted because I was so lonely. I know that if Grandad had been alive, he'd have told me to run for the hills and never look back.

My eyes blur with tears as I recall that night, that horrible night, when I lost a baby for a second time. He'd come home from one of his so-called business dinners, and I knew he'd been with someone else. Now I know that person was Nicky. I could smell her perfume on his clothes, even over the reek of whisky.

I asked him who he'd been with. I knew I shouldn't have, but I said it anyway. He slapped me hard across my face, knocking me off balance, and I fell to the floor. He screamed at me never to question him again about where he'd been or who he'd been with. I was too scared to answer back. I was always too scared because I never knew what his mood would be, or how he was going to react. He continued hitting me while I lay on the floor. He kept shouting at me: *Are you listening? You're my wife, you belong to me, and you'll do as you're told.*

I nodded silently, agreeing with him, hoping that he'd stop beating me, but he didn't. I tried so hard to protect my baby, putting my hands over my belly, whimpering, begging him to stop, but he just laughed at me. He loomed over me, pulling my hair, shouting and slapping me. He dragged me upstairs by my hair and threw me on the bed. I landed hard on my tummy.

He walked away, drunk and muttering, "That'll fucking teach her to disobey me."

I wished then that he'd fall down the stairs and break his neck. How could he hit me while I was pregnant?

Later that night, in the hospital, I lost the most precious thing to me in the world – another baby.

They gave me pills to take home for the pain, and I sat with them in my hand and wondered, if I took them all would it stop? Would this misery end? Gran was with me – she'd taken me because Adam was too drunk – and she smiled at me as I thought those terrible things, not knowing what I was thinking.

She put her arm around me and kissed my forehead, and I felt ashamed of what I was thinking, because I knew deep down I couldn't put her through that; I loved her too much. She wiped the tears from my eyes as she'd done when I was a child, and unknowingly, with that smile and gesture of love towards me, she saved my life that night, just as she had when

I was four years old and she'd taken me home after the death of my parents and loved me like she did. I often wonder if she really knew what I was thinking that night, and what she would have done if she had known.

I went home, depressed, lonely and empty – thinking it was my fault I'd lost my second baby, just as I'd blamed myself for the loss of my first child. He'd hit me just the once when he found out, but the shouting and the mind games increased dramatically until I miscarried through stress – the hospital nearly said as much. But the second time, the beating, that was his fault. He didn't care, never even asked me how I was or about the baby he'd known I'd lost because of his monstrous actions. I never spoke about it after that night. I never told my gran, or the hospital, what had really happened. Instead I said I fell. I tried to block out as much of that night as I possibly could, burying my head in the sand, hoping the pain would eventually stop. It never did.

I turn my head sharply away from the pills, and catch sight of the photo of my family I've brought with me. They smile out from the frame at me, and I feel so much love for them as I recall what Gran said to me when I was a child, after my parents were killed.

When you're sad, try to think a happy thought.

I used to think of ice cream, and ponies, holidays with my mum and dad, but such innocent thoughts aren't strong enough any more. So I try hard to think a happy thought. I smile at the photo, and I realise that it's been there since the day I was born. And there she is, smiling back at me from the photo. My gran.

Chapter 8

I take a deep breath. I really need to get out of here and rid myself of these thoughts that are swimming about in my head, of Adam and Nicky. I walk over to my bag, pull out my trainers and sweatshirt and put them on. My other clothes are left scattered over the floor. I leave the flat in a hurry, desperate to clear my head.

It's chilly and dark outside. I start walking, breathing in deeply with every step. It's colder than I'd expected, and I can see my breath in front of me, so I pick up speed, walking faster. Then I start to run. The harder I run, the quicker my head clears, so I push on. Once I start, I can't stop. My legs are hurting, but it feels good. I start to relax as I'm concentrate on the sound of my feet pounding the pavement. Leaving the thought of Adam and Nicky behind me and I've no idea where I am, or where I'm running to. I just know I need to keep going.

It's dark and it's starting to rain. The wind's picked up speed and it's freezing cold and icy against my skin. I've been running for at least an hour when I have to stop abruptly and inhale deeply. I've a stitch in my side that takes my breath away. My legs are wobbly now I've stopped, and I start to feel sick. I gasp for air, then vomit into the gutter.

"I hate being sick," I moan. I've hardly any energy left. I feel weak and suddenly dizzy, so I sit myself down on the kerbside and look around. I've still no idea where I am. There are houses behind me and fields in front of me, but I'm still on the main road. I'm soaked with sweat. It's freezing cold, and I start to shiver.

A car speeds past me. Water from the spray of the tyres hits me in the face. I screw my eyes shut and cover my face with my hands, feeling very sorry for myself. I start thinking again about Adam and Nicky, and her being pregnant. It's making my head spin. All I can see is her face laughing at me, gloating as she rubs her bump. Then Adam's manipulative words float over me, trying to consume me, trying to get back into my mind, and I feel as though I'm falling apart again.

But this time I shock myself. I shout, "No!", shaking my head as if I'm trying to dislodge him from my thoughts.

I get to my feet, still a little wobbly, but now I can feel a clench in my jaw. I'm getting angry as I remember what he's like, what he's done to me. He's selfish and cruel.

Well, no more! He can hit me, punch me, slap me, but I'm never going back to him. I recall his words. *We can work things out.* Like hell we can. I'm going to deal with him once and for all. I should have left him months ago, that dreadful night after the loss of my baby, but I was in such a dark place then. Not that I'm in a brilliant place now, but I'm better than I was. He wants my house and my money. He wants everything to stay the same, with me doing what I'm told like a good little girl. No, no more. I'm not going to allow myself to go back to that ever again. I'm worth more than that, worth more than him, and worth more than Nicky. I've come too far, and I can't let him rule me or ruin my life any longer. I still miss my babies so very much, and I know I'll never get over the loss of them, but I have to move on. I need to do this. I *can* do this. I can change myself and my life.

I stand at the side of the road, still unsteady but nevertheless determined. I turn around and head towards the flat, retracing my steps, hoping I can find my way back. I'm not running fast, because I'm shattered and gasping for breath. Every muscle hurts, and my lungs feel like they're about to burst. I concentrate on running more slowly, just to get back in one piece.

And for the first time in four years, I know what I'm doing. I'm taking a stand, and it feels marvellous.

I eventually arrive back at the flat. There's a police car in the car park, but I don't pay much attention to it as I punch in the key code and walk up the corridor. The door's open. I look at it, puzzled, because I'm certain I closed it behind me. I walk inside and lean against the wall, my legs like jelly from the exertion. I kick off my trainers, pulling a face at myself. I stink. I'm covered in sick and dripping with sweat. I need a shower.

I close the door behind me, shouting to Alison, "Hi, I'm back."

There's no answer. I quickly check the flat, but she's not here. All the doors are open. I check the clock: 10.30 p.m. God, I've been gone hours. No wonder I'm knackered.

I walk towards the kitchen, noticing my pill bottle sitting near the phone on the little side table. Strange, I think to myself, but I carry on to the kitchen without thinking any more of it. I need water. I grab a glass off the shelf and fill it from the tap. I have a long drink, then head towards the bathroom. I turn on the shower and strip off my wet things.

The hot water against my skin feels amazing. I place a generous blob of shower gel on the sponge and start lathering it over my skin. I let the water cascade over my head, feeling a wave of dizziness wash over me. Then a trickle of blood runs down the side of my face. I put my hand to my head, but everything is starting to spin. I try to sit down, slowly sliding myself down the glass door and leaving a trail of blood where my hand has been.

The water is so hot that it's slightly opened the dressing to the wound on my forehead, and blood oozes down my face. I slump heavily on the floor of the shower and sit very still, letting the water run over me, trying to compose myself, waiting for the dizziness to pass as I don't want to slip and suffer another bang to my head. I start to heave again, but there's no food in my stomach, just bile, and it hurts as I retch.

The bloods making me feel worse, and there's so much of it. I'm light-headed and a little disorientated. I feel as though I'm going to pass out. I tell myself to sit still, that it will pass, that it's just fatigue. I've done too much, too soon.

I'm huddled over, cradling my legs with my arms,

breathing deeply through my mouth, trying to stay calm, but I'm starting to feel faint.

The bathroom door flies open and bangs against the wall, making me jump.

I can hear Edward's voice shouting, "She's here! In the shower!"

He prises open the shower door and crouches over me, dragging me out by my arms. I fall into his lap, vaguely aware that Alison is shouting almost hysterically in the background.

"Is she all right? Is she alive?"

I don't understand what's going on. I feel dizzy and panicky. Edward moves my hair away from my face. His voice is raised, but calm.

"Abigail, how many have you taken?"

I don't answer him. I don't know what he's talking about, or what's happening. His face is too close to mine.

"How many? How many?"

I'm so confused.

"Answer me!"

Alison darts into the bathroom. "Oh my God! What has she done?" she says, almost screaming.

Edwards turns to her, and gives her a look that makes her fall silent.

"Where's Tom?" he asks her calmly.

"He's coming," she replies, flustered. "He's on his way."

"Ask him to come into the bathroom when he gets here," he replies.

I move forward, reaching for a towel since I'm sitting naked on his knee. Edward grabs the towel and places it over me, whispering, "What have you done?"

He takes my wrist, feeling my pulse while looking into my eyes. I feel woozy and sick, and the room's spinning again. I think I'm going to pass out. I hear two voices in the lounge, muffled, as if they're underwater.

"Miss Bridge, you called us?"

I can hear a static noise, like a radio.

"She's in there, in the bathroom. Mr Scott is with her. He's a surgeon from the hospital, and my boyfriend's on his way. He's also a doctor."

"Miss Bridge, are these the pills?"

"Yes."

There's a pause and I hear Tom shout, "Alison!"

"Oh, Tom, you're here."

"Miss Bridge!"

Alison's voice is panicked as she replies, "Sorry, sorry. She's in the bathroom with Edward, Mr Scott, I mean. Oh, Tom, I hope she's going to be okay. She's not talking and she looks dreadful."

"Is she all right? How many pills did she take?"

"I don't know. She's dazed, she's not spoken. And there's blood everywhere."

Pills? I haven't taken any pills. I can't seem to concentrate, or find the words to speak.

"Blood?" I hear Tom ask. He hurries to the bathroom. "Edward, is she all right?"

A police officer follows Tom into the bathroom. I try to get up, but I feel strange.

"I think she's all right," Edward says, his voice tense. "I don't know how many pills she's taken. Her pulse is normal, and there's no mydriasis, but I can't be sure because she hasn't spoken."

"Abigail, have you taken any pills?" Tom asks slowly.

I frown.

A second police officer is talking to Alison in the lounge. I have no idea what's happening. Everyone is talking, asking me questions that I can't make any sense of. I was in the shower when I felt strange, then Edward was dragging me out. Now the police are here. Everyone keeps asking me about pills. What pills?

The policeman walks over to me. I try to pull myself together as he kneels down.

"Abigail ..."

I stare at him.

"Can you tell me, have you taken any of these?" He holds the pill bottle in front of me.

I just shake my head.

"And the blood?"

I point to my head.

He looks at the wound and nods. "You're certain about the pills? You've not taken any?"

I don't feel very well, and I hate that all these people are in the room, talking and shouting, asking me questions that I don't know the answers to. I'm naked, with just a towel wrapped around me, sitting on Edward's knee. I just want everyone to leave.

I finally find my voice and snap, "Yes! God, stop asking me questions. Please ..." I turn to look at Edward. "What the hell is going on?"

He seems pleased that I'm speaking, and he raises his eyes.

"Thank God, she's speaking."

He pulls me close to him, and I don't know if he's concerned or chastising me. He's holding me too tightly and I feel trapped. I still don't understand what's going on, and it's scaring me.

"Stop it," I shout. "Please, let me get up." But I sound angrier than I mean to.

He sighs as the police officer holds out his hand to me. I take it, holding onto the towel tightly, but as I stand I feel my legs wobble. I grab for the wall to steady myself. Edward jumps to his feet behind me, grabbing me before I fall backwards.

"Are you okay?" the police officer asks, concerned.

I nod.

"Do you want to be checked over at the hospital?"

Edward frowns at him.

"Sorry, Mr Scott, you've done that already, I know, but I need to ask Abigail."

Edward has stopped glaring now, but his reply is firm. I think he's a little put out by the police officer's remark.

"I have checked her over, yes, and I can assure you that she just needs to get some rest." He sounds cross.

The policeman merely nods his head towards Edward, asking, "Can we leave her in your capable hands then, Mr Scott?"

"Yes, you can. That's fine." He still sounds angry. "Thank you for being so prompt. I think I'm quite capable of looking after her now."

I look at the police officer and roll my eyes. He nods at me, ignores Edward, and leaves the bathroom.

The police speak to Alison in the lounge before they leave, and she apologises to them for calling them out.

"It's better to be safe than sorry, Miss Bridge," one replies pleasantly. "Don't worry. Your friend's going to be all right."

"She is? Oh, thank you!"

The police officers leave, and we all stand in silence for a moment. My dizziness is passing, although I still feel confused. I look at Edward, and I'm mortified to see that his clothes are wet, and his shirt is covered in my blood.

"I'm sorry!" I gasp.

He shakes his head and holds out his hand. I take it, holding on to the towel with my other hand. He walks me out of the bathroom. Alison and Tom watch us go and I smile at them uncertainly, a little bewildered and embarrassed by the whole situation. I'm guessing they thought I'd taken the pills, and what with all the blood … it must have looked bad.

Alison smiles back at me and then moves to hug me, apologising, but Tom takes her hand and shakes his head at her.

"Give them a minute," he says to her quietly. She nods at him, then smiles at me again.

"I'm fine," I say. "Honestly."

"Can I just have five minutes, please, Abigail?" Edward asks.

I nod, and he leads me into my room.

"I need to put some clothes on," I point out.

"Yes, sorry."

I pick up a top and a pair of shorts from the floor, and wait for Edward to turn his back before putting them on. When I'm finished, I sit on the bed and study his back, wondering why he's here. He turns to face me.

"You scared me," he states flatly.

"I did?" I say, taken aback.

"Yes!"

"I'm sorry, I didn't mean to. Why are you here, anyway?"

His face darkens at my question, but I hadn't meant to sound so aggressive.

"Why the empty pill bottle?"

I frown at his accusatory tone.

"I couldn't get the lid off so I threw it at the wall in a temper."

He shakes his head at me dismissively.

"You were missing for three hours."

I'm annoyed, and a little put out that I should have to answer to him all of a sudden.

"What are you implying?" I ask defensively.

"The pill bottle? Missing for three hours? What do you think I'm implying?"

"I don't know or I wouldn't be asking, would I?"

"You've not answered my question," he goads, and he sounds so pompous that I want to stick my tongue out at him. He's being a Richard Cranium again.

"And you've not answered my question," I snap back.

"Oh, for God's sake, Abigail, how old are you? You're being childish now."

I'm fuming; I want to knock his bloody head off! Childish?

"Really? I'm not the one playing games. If you've got something to say, then either spit it out or leave." I'm not childish, I'm mad. I huff and wave my arms about. "In fact, I think you'd better just leave before I say something I regret."

He looks surprised.

"I beg your pardon?"

"You heard me."

"I'll just leave then, shall I?"

"I think that's what I just said, or are you deaf as well as stupid?" I pull a face and mimic him. *"For God's sake, Abigail, how old are you?"* I curl my lips into a sneer. *"That* was childish."

He looks annoyed, but I don't care and it's not like we're seeing each other.

"Well, I'm sorry for caring."

He starts to leave, but at the door he turns and walks back quickly. I shake my head.

"I told you to leave!"

"No, I want to stay."

I shake my head again, but he takes hold of my hands.

"Please let go of my hands," I say as calmly as I can. "I want you to leave"

He looks at me and his eyes, usually so sexy, are clouded with sadness. I think I've hurt his feelings. My heart beats faster, and I'm not certain if I feel angry or upset. I gasp as he suddenly pulls me towards him, holding my wrists. It takes me by surprise and I stumble forward into his chest. His grip is so strong that I can't move, and the feeling of being powerless leaves me scared. It's not the kind of fear that Adam instils in me, but fear of the intensity of my feelings towards him.

I let out a deep sigh. "Please … you need to leave."

He shakes his head at me, his reply soft.

"I don't want to leave."

"Please let me go," I say quietly.

He continues to hold me, and it makes me feel dizzy. He moves to kiss my cheek, and I close my eyes. I want him to kiss me, and I want to kiss him back, but I can't. I'm too scared.

"Stop," I whisper, my voice hoarse. "You need to leave." I

don't want him to leave, of course; I like him. I like that he makes me feel as if I'm truly alive, but it's not right. I whisper again. "Stop, please." But again I'm ignored. I raise my voice. "Please, Edward, just stop."

My heart beats so fast that I feel faint. My emotions are spiralling through me at breakneck speed. But he lets go of me, the surprise evident on his face. I don't think many women have told him to stop, but I really can't do this, not now.

"You really want me to leave?" he asks, and I nod my head.

I want to explain, but I can't find the words.

"You want me to go right now?"

I bite my lip hard and squeeze my eyes shut as I lower my head, because I know that if I look into his eyes I'll ask him to stay. I nod my head.

"Fine!" he says, curtly. "I'll leave."

"I'm sorry," I whisper, but I don't think he's heard me as he stalks towards the door. He opens it, walks through and slams it behind him. It makes me jump and I cover my face with my hands. I can hear Tom asking him if he wants a drink, and he snaps a reply.

"No, I'm leaving … apparently."

The front door opens, then closes with a bang. I hear a muffled conversation, presumably about what's just happened between Edward and me. They must have heard everything.

There's a knock at my bedroom door, and Alison pops her head in.

"Can I come in?"

I nod, and she smiles hesitantly.

"Edward's just come back. He's asking to see you. What would you like me to say to him?"

"I don't know," I reply truthfully. "I'm confused."

"Do you want to see him? Talk to him?"

I put my hands to my face again.

"Honestly?"

She nods.

"I don't know what I want. If he comes in, I'll say all the wrong things. I can't think straight when he's here. I don't say what I mean. He flusters me."

"Do you want me to say that you'll speak to him tomorrow? When your head is a little clearer."

"Yes, please," I say gratefully. "Thanks."

"No problem."

She heads back to the lounge and I hear her speaking. "I'm sorry, but she said she'll speak to you tomorrow. She's really upset, what with everything that has happened."

I imagine him sighing, but when he speaks his voice is curt, even through the door. I know his anger isn't aimed at Alison. It's aimed at me.

"Fine!"

And I hear him leave once again.

Chapter 9

I breathe heavily as I climb into bed, feeling drained by the whole strange evening. Alison pops her head back into my room, but I don't give her a chance to speak.

"I heard. He sounded really cross."

She smiles and says nothing, which is all the confirmation I need. But I've problems of my own that I need to figure out, and this definitely wasn't the right time or place. "Thank you," I add, "and I'm truly sorry about tonight."

"You've nothing to apologise for. I'm sorry I read the situation all wrong and called the police. Edward was really upset when Tom rang him."

"Tom rang him?" I say, surprised.

She nods her head slowly.

"And told him what?"

She bites her lip and takes a deep breath.

"I'm sorry, I thought you knew." She smiles nervously. "He told him everything, I think."

I close my eyes, shaking my head, not at Alison, but at the situation. It's such a mess.

"I am really sorry," she continues anxiously. "I was scared. I didn't know what to do. When Tom and I came back to the flat, we saw the empty pill bottle in your room, and there was no sign of you. After what I'd heard you say at your house …" She closes her eyes. "I thought … you'd done something daft."

I study her face. She seems genuinely upset. I suppose she was only doing what any good friend would do. I concede it must have looked bad.

"It's okay, really. This isn't your fault. It's his."

"Whose? Edward's, for coming round?"

"No! If anything it was good of Edward to come round, and then search the streets for me. Although I don't quite understand why he'd do that when he barely knows me."

"I can."

I raise my eyebrows at her.

"Because he likes you," she goes on. "He dropped everything and came straight over when Tom called him, and when you didn't come back he went straight out to look for you. I think he was scared, although he didn't actually say as much. Did you manage to talk with him, straighten it out?"

I shake my head. "I heard you and Tom talking, and I've heard the other nurses talking about his reputation. He's a one-night stand man, only out to get what he wants. What did Tom say? Shag them, then leave them. I'm not on the market to boost a man's ego."

Alison nods reluctantly.

"And I've had my fill off bossy, domineering men."

"I'm sorry."

"It's fine. I just need to get myself together and stop Adam from getting inside my head. Yes, Edward's handsome and charming, and of course I fancy him, a little more than I ought to, but I've fallen for that before and look where it got me. Once bitten, twice shy."

"God, I know what you mean. Yes, you're right." She hesitates. "Can I ask you something? I'm not prying, honestly, but has Adam, you know, hurt you?" I know she doesn't mean my feelings, but this isn't the right time.

"I'm really sorry, I don't want to talk about it, not now anyway."

I get the feeling that she wishes she hadn't asked.

"Yeah, yeah, sorry. I didn't mean to—" She sighs. "I'm not being nosey – I was just trying to, you know …"

She's obviously flustered, and I feel suddenly guilty. I take her hand.

"Please, it's not you or Edward, or anyone else for that matter, making me feel like this. I just need some time to myself to get my head around everything that's happened. I'm stronger now than I've ever been. I know it might not seem like that to you, but, believe me, I am. And that's down to you helping me the way you have, letting me stay here with you so I don't have to face him. I can finally start to sort my life out."

"Do you mean that? Because the last thing I want to do is to add to your problems, or upset you more."

"I mean it. It's okay, honestly. Please don't worry about me." I smile at her, "I'm made of sturdier stuff, you know."

She smiles back at me.

"I know Tom feels bad about ringing Edward and asking him to come over, especially when you'd already said that you didn't want to speak to him."

"Never mind," I say, rolling my eyes a little. "It's done now. Tell him not to feel bad. I suppose he was just doing what he thought was best, that's all."

"Yes, I believe he was."

I fall silent. I know I've over-reacted to the situation, but the fact is I struggle to trust people. Maybe Edward is actually really nice, maybe he really is a genuine person, but I don't think I'm strong enough to find out right now. I know I can't take much more heartache at the moment. It's not Adam or Nicky, or leaving my marriage. It's not even his threats, because I've suffered a great deal more than that at his hand. It's these memories of my lost babies that have returned to haunt me. Seeing Nicky pregnant has brought it all back, and I can't talk about that to anyone.

"I'm sorry, but if you don't mind then I think I'm just going to try and get some sleep."

"Gosh, no, not at all. I'll leave you to it. Do you need anything?"

"No, I'm fine, thanks."

"Okay. I'll see you in the morning then."

Once she's gone, I make myself comfortable on the bed and drift off to sleep.

It's morning when I wake. I yawn, still feeling exhausted. I've been disturbed all night by strange dreams about Adam,

Edward, Tom and Alison. I can't remember them properly – they're vague and jumbled up – but I know I dreamt about that awful night with Adam when I lost my baby; then Edward was there, and Tom and Alison, and we were here in the flat, dancing. Edward and I were dating, and we were happy. Adam and Nicky were just a distant memory.

I put my hands to my face, wondering if I'm having a breakdown, and catch the wound on my forehead. I mutter to myself. I sit up in bed and notice blood on my pillow. I wander over to the mirror and look at myself – the dressing is coming off. I lift it slightly to look underneath; the Steri-Strips are loose. I walk into the lounge to see if Alison is up yet, and whether she has another dressing.

"Morning!" I point to my head. "Do you have another dressing I could borrow, please?"

"I'll ask Tom to look at it for you," she says with a warm smile.

"He seems lovely," I comment.

She giggles. "Well, I like him!"

"Have you been seeing each other long?"

"Hmm … four months, two weeks and three days."

"Not that you're counting then."

She laughs, and calls out to him. Tom comes into the lounge; he's already dressed for work in pale-blue scrubs. He smiles at me, and I notice for the first time how handsome he is. His blue eyes are lovely, and they look kind. This brings on a memory from my dream – of Edward and how he looked at me with those seductive, heavy-lidded eyes of his. Sleepy, come-to-bed eyes with long, dark eyelashes that lure you in, like a moth to a flame. I feel my cheeks blush at the thought.

"Let's take a look then," Tom says. "Umm … It needs redoing. You'd better call onto the ward and let Edward reattach new Steri-Strips and a dressing."

I don't want Edward to do it. I don't think I can face him, not after last night. I'd feel too awkward.

"Can't you do it, please?"

Tom looks at Alison and then at me. I think I've put him on the spot.

"I'd better not. I don't want to step on Edward's toes. Sorry! Alison, have you got any tape? I'll fasten the old dressing down for you."

She nods, then pulls some tape from a drawer and passes it to him.

I wince as he secures the dressing.

"Sorry, is it sore?"

I nod, rolling my eyes at him.

He smiles sympathetically. "There, all done."

"Thank you," I say.

"I'd better be off. I'll see you tonight, Alison."

Alison smiles warmly at Tom – bless her, she has it bad!

She turns to me. "I'll come with you to the ward if you want, Abbie?"

I nod, knowing she's kind.

"Please, if you don't mind. I'll just wash and get dressed."

I leave them alone to say their goodbyes and head to the bathroom to wash. Then return to my bedroom and pull my jeans on. I realise they're quite loose around my waist. I roll my eyes. I need to start taking better care of myself. I've not been eating properly over the past few months. I pull in my belt a notch. I see how flat my tummy is as I'm looking in the mirror, and run my hand over it. I must be a size eight now, if that. I pick up my bra from the floor and put it on. I've not lost any weight from my boobs – still a 34D. I'm blessed with the Baxter genes, as Gran would say. If I lose any more weight, I'll have to stop running for fear of falling over, top heavy.

I smile as I realise that I look like my mum in the photos I have of her when she was young. My hair's not as dark as hers; it's more chestnut, with strands of reddish brown running through it, which makes it shine, like my gran's hair used to. It's wavy and thick, hard to manage, which is why I keep it long. I hardly ever wear it loose; mostly I tie it up or put it in a ponytail – it's easier to deal with that way.

I grab a T-shirt and my white jumper from the floor, noticing the pills underneath them. I pull a face. That's why they thought I'd taken the tablets; my clothes were hiding them. I put on my Converses, tie my hair up in a ponytail, and head for the lounge to wait for Alison.

"I'm ready, Alison! Thanks for coming with me. I don't think I could face him on my own, not after last night. I behaved quite …" I finish my sentence with a sigh, thinking of Edward and what happened.

"You were upset. It's understandable. God, if I'd been through half of what you have, well … Come on. Let's go and get your head sorted out."

"Cheers, but I think it'll take a lot more than tape to sort my head out."

Her eyes widen, and she laughs. "I didn't mean it like that!"

"I know what you meant," I say. "Sorry, I just think I'm a little nervous."

I grab my bag as we leave the flat.

We arrive on the ward, and most of the staff are in the handover. My heart is drumming away in my chest and I feel jittery again. We take a seat near the nurses' station and wait for the handover to finish. I watch the clock: 7.45 a.m., 7.46 a.m., 7.47 a.m. I let out a deep breath, feeling nervous.

"I'm just going to the toilet …" I mouth. "I need a wee."

Alison nods, and I make my way into the staff toilets to use the loo.

My hands are shaking as I wash them, and I feel hot and flushed. I'm acting like a silly schoolgirl, just because I'm nervous about seeing him. He affects me badly, but I know he isn't right for me. He's gorgeous, clever and funny, but he's also arrogant and controlling, a one-night stand man, a player. He could hurt me so badly, and I'm not in the market for that. I try to resign myself to the fact that we should just be friends, although I don't think he'll be feeling too friendly towards me after last night. I leave the toilets and return to find Alison.

"Are you okay?" she asks.

I nod. "Yes, I'm fine."

Yvonne, the housekeeper, walks past and smiles cheerfully.

"Hi, girls," she says, glancing at my head. "That looks nasty! Have you come to get it re-dressed?"

"Yes. The dressing came off in the shower."

The door to the staff room opens and everyone pours out, walking onto the ward. They're all busy talking to each other, but I see one or two of them glance in our direction and then jerk their heads to one side as if to say, *Look who's here!* Great, I'll be the talk of the ward again. I bet Facebook had a right bashing last night. I'm so glad I'm not on it.

Sister walks up the ward with Darcy and spots us. I stand up straighter as soon as she starts in our direction. She makes me so nervous that I want to salute her. Darcy throws me a dirty look, and I wonder what's eating her. She walks behind the nurses' station, still throwing me the daggers. Oh, I've made such a great impression, I think to myself.

"What do you want?" Sister says, her voice stern. "I thought you were off sick this week."

I'm about to answer her when she looks away, smiling at Alison.

"Alison, can you do a late shift for me today, please? It appears we're short-staffed."

That was a dig if ever there was one.

"Yes, that's fine, I can do that, Sister, but Tom has told Abbie to come and get her head re-dressed by Mr Scott."

Sister raises an eyebrow at Alison. She knows that Tom is a doctor, and she wouldn't dream of disobeying a senior doctor; she's too old school for that. She still barks back at us though – I think just to remind us that she's our senior and we've to do as she says. I'm right at the bottom of the pecking order, and she wants me to know it.

"Well, Mr Scott is busy." She shouts to Darcy, and points

to my forehead. "Darcy, see to this!"

This? Charming! Darcy moves away from the nurses' station and towards me, huffing as she looks me up and down.

"This way," she remarks snidely.

I roll my eyes at Alison, who grimaces and mimics Darcy. *"This way!"* Then she says calmly, "I'll wait here."

I smirk, mouthing back to her, "Thanks."

Yvonne hovers a little longer, watching me and looking puzzled as I follow Miss Personality of the Year into the treatment room.

When we're alone, she snaps, "Sit!"

She's so nasty, and I wonder where she did her training – SS Boot Camp? She's got the bedside manner of a warthog. She grabs a dressing pack off the shelf, opens it, puts on the gloves and walks over to me with a surly look on her face. Without saying a word, she reaches out and rips the dressing off my head. The pain makes me gasp, and I pull my lips in tight. She grins, and I want to scream, *You bitch!* She then grabs one of the Steri-Strips and pulls it off quickly. *Shit, that hurt.* I sit on my hands, gritting my teeth and glaring at her. She's clearly loving every second of this. She goes to grab another one, and I shut my eyes tight as she rips it hard from my head.

"Ow!" Tears prick my eyes and a trickle of blood runs down my cheek.

"Shut up," she sneers nastily. "Don't be so pathetic. You're acting like a baby."

I want to punch her, the cow! Don't be so pathetic? I jump as the door opens, and glance up to see Edward standing in the doorway. I've tears welling in my eyes from the pain, and the blood is running down my face and onto my white jumper. Darcy ignores it and turns to see who's entered the room. When she realises who it is, her face flushes an ugly shade of red. Her voice drops, becoming soft and flirtatious.

"Mr Scott. Hi, do you want me?"

His eyes are locked on mine, and he looks mystified as to why I'm bleeding.

"Why is Abigail bleeding?" he asks Darcy coldly. She looks at him and stammers, her face flushing redder as she tries to think of an explanation for her behaviour.

"Umm … umm … they were stuck," she finishes lamely.

I frown, raising my eyebrows. Is that the best she can come up with? Edward isn't convinced either.

"Then why didn't you wet them before removing them?"

I wipe my eyes as the blood starts to trickle into them. He sees me doing this, and reaches over to pass me a tissue. She huffs, but Edward hears her and his face creases into a scowl.

"Go and find Sister. Tell her to come here immediately."

She's livid, and looks like she's going to cry. She glares at me behind his back, mouthing, "You bitch." She storms past me, knocking into me on purpose, before leaving the room.

Seconds later, Sister enters the room. She looks at Edward, then at me, and then back at him again. No one says anything. Edward finally breaks the silence.

"Sister, can you please re-dress Abigail's wound?"

She nods, looking at me. She sees the blood, and just for a moment her face shows a flash of compassion and she almost seems human.

I tear my eyes away from her as Edward starts to leave the room without speaking to me. He's clearly still angry with me about last night, for telling him to leave; I can sense it. Why else would he not be doing the dressing himself, like he did before? I need to apologise about last night, if only to say a simple sorry. His hand is on the door handle, his back is to me.

I call his name timidly. "Mr Scott?"

He turns to look at me, his eyes no longer sad or angry, but back to come-to-bed, and they draw me in so fast, beckoning me closer. Once again, I find myself unable to speak to him. It's absurd – I can't draw the words from my mouth.

Sister's eyes dart between us as she waits for someone to speak. I'm stupidly flustered again. God, why can't I do this? Why does he affect me this way? He watches me, waiting for me to say something, and when I don't his expression grows aggrieved.

I sigh and stare at my lap.

He lets out an impatient huff.

"Get her some tablets for the pain, and please make sure they're in a box. She seems to struggle with the lids on bottles. Thank you, Sister."

I scowl at him, but he turns and leaves the room.

That was uncalled for. Was he waiting for me to apologise? Well, he can whistle bloody Dixie now. God, he likes to get his own way; what he wants, when he wants it. He's utterly draining.

I sit in silence while Sister redoes the dressing on my head, although I'm seething inside at his parting remark. She finishes quickly, but when I thank her she rolls her eyes.

"Sister, I know we're short-staffed, so please can I come back to work tomorrow?"

"Do you feel up to it?"

I nod. "Yes."

"Okay, come in on an early shift." I smile at her, although it isn't acknowledged. Instead, her voice turns inquisitive. "Abigail, is there something going on between you and Mr Scott?"

"No! Not at all," I reply matter-of-factly. Apart from the fact that he annoys and provokes me, I add silently.

"Good," she says firmly, although I'm not sure she believes me.

She turns and leaves the room, with me trailing behind her. Alison is waiting for me outside.

"What happened in there?" she asks when Sister is out of earshot. "Darcy came bursting out and called for Sister, and then Sister went running back into the treatment room. Darcy went and hid in the toilet! Her face was as red as beetroot, and it looked like she was crying. And then when Mr Scott came out, he looked furious."

"I don't know," I reply, shaking my head. "It's him. He's so arrogant and self-absorbed. Everyone has to do what he says or face the full force of his wrath."

Alison frowns at me.

"What? It's true. You saw what he was like last night, just because I asked him to leave—"

"Abbie," she interrupts, rolling her eyes.

"Well, he is." I'm on a roll now. "He's domineering and up his own arse. He flusters me and scares me. I know exactly what his problem is – he doesn't like to be told no."

"Abbie!"

"What?" I cry, frustrated now.

Her eyes are like saucers as she stares over my shoulder. I feel bile rising in my throat, as I suddenly realise what she's been trying to tell me.

I mouth to her, "He's behind me, isn't he?"

She nods, and I close my eyes.

"Damn!" I mutter.

I turn slowly and find him watching me with a sullen expression. I make a gurgling noise in my throat; I'm momentarily too embarrassed to speak.

"That was a different Mr Scott," I add feebly, trying my best to worm my way out of the situation.

His face is impassive, and I know it's not going to work. I want the ground to swallow me up, and I feel my face burning.

"How long have you been standing there?" I manage to ask ruefully.

He doesn't look amused at all.

"Long enough."

"I'm sorry, I didn't—"

He puts his hand up to silence me, not giving me a chance to explain. He spins around without another word, and I watch him leave the ward in silence. I want to kick myself. I didn't mean any of that, I really didn't. I feel terrible now. He must think I'm a first-class bitch. He'd said that he would see me later today, but I don't think that's going to happen now.

I don't say anything to Alison as we leave the ward. Not speaking seems like the best option, as I can't seem to keep my foot out of my mouth when I open it. I keep smiling at Alison and wondering what on earth she must think of me now.

Chapter 10

We arrive back at Alison's flat. As we step through the door, I shake my head at her and she bursts out laughing. I start to giggle with her. I'm not sure why, but it's better than crying.

"Oh Lord!" I say, wiping tears from my eyes. "I can honestly say, with my hand on my heart, that I've never in my whole life gotten myself into so much trouble as I have done these past few days. I wish I'd never come here! Is it always like this?"

She shakes her head at me.

"Oh, so it's just me then?"

"Yes, just you!"

"Thanks for the confidence boost."

"But I'm so glad you did come here. We're going to have so much fun, you and I!"

"Fun?" I look sceptical. "I've not seen much of that since I arrived here."

"How long do you want to stay?"

"Is a week or so okay? Just until I get my head around things."

"Stay as long as you want, and I mean that. Are you feeling any better about things? I'm not prying, honestly. I'm just concerned about you."

"I'll be okay. I just need some time to sort things out. My head mainly," I say, although I know I'll never get over what happened that night. But Adam I can sort out, and I will.

She smiles, and doesn't ask any more. Instead she changes the subject.

"What are you going to do today?"

"I think I'd better clean my room for starters. What are you up to?"

"Nothing this morning. I'm meeting Tom later for lunch, and then I'm doing that late shift."

"Oh, yeah," I say, pulling a face. "Sorry about that."

"It's all right," she says, grinning. "It'll give me some brownie points with Sister."

"God, I could do with a whole lot of brownie points with that woman. I think she hates me! And Darcy – what's her problem?"

Alison raises her eyebrows at me.

"You've not cottoned on to that one yet, have you?"

"No," I say, thinking about it for a moment. Then I ask. "Who, Sister?"

"No!" she says, shaking her head. "Sister's okay, once you get to know her. She runs a tight ship, and likes things done right."

I shrug, still not sure what she's talking about.

"No, seriously, I think you may have just upset the apple cart a little."

"Yes, I probably did," I laugh. "I've plunged her ward into chaos, and seeing that I'm going back to work tomorrow, it'll no doubt be the same."

"No not that. I mean Darcy, with Edward. She's infatuated with him. She's been trying to snare him for ages according to Tom. She's been with loads of doctors at the hospital, so I believe. We all know she's very attractive – anyone can see that – but they all seem to dump her in the end. Edward's never, you know, *entertained* her. He's not interested, despite all her efforts. She's desperate to go with him. She never stops talking about him, always asking questions and trying to find out where he goes and what he does outside of the hospital. Tom says she's even dated some of Edward's friends to try to get close to him. It seems like he's her ultimate conquest, and, according to the gossip on the wards, she's jealous as hell about the way he's reacted to you."

"Wow, I can't understand why they'd dump her, can you?" I say sarcastically. "As you say, she's very attractive, and she's got a fantastic personality as well. It makes you wonder how some people's minds work." I pull a face at Alison and we burst into laughter. "I'm staying well clear of that psycho, thank you very much! And as for Edward, I think that's a no-go area."

She ignores my last comment and smiles at me.

"You're much prettier than Darcy."

"I don't think so."

"What? Are you kidding me? You're a natural beauty. I don't think you see what everyone else sees when you look in the mirror."

I shake my head. When I look in the mirror, I just see me; plain, sad, confused, angry, lonely Abbie, with enough heartache to last a lifetime. But I don't say any of that.

"Don't be daft! You're making me blush."

"Just telling it like it is. Tom said a lot of the male staff are talking about you."

"Get out of here!"

"It's true. And as for Edward, well, according to Tom, it's unheard of for him to chase any woman. They usually just fall at his feet and roll over. That's how he expects every woman to behave around him."

I laugh. "I don't think so somehow."

"Well, you don't have to take my word for it. Just ask Tom."

I chuckle to myself as I go to my room. I fold my things and put them away in the drawers and the wardrobe. I make my bed and gently place the rabbit on my pillow. Then I get down on my hands and knees and do my best to pick all the pills up off the floor, all the while shaking my head and remembering Edward's words. *Make sure they're in a box.* I snort jeeringly, thinking, *Sarcastic sod.*

Alison pops her head into my room.

"I'm off now. I'll see you tonight."

"Okay. Have a nice lunch with Tom."

"Thanks, I will! Bye."

By the time I've finished my room and secured the last of

the pills in their bottle, I feel like some fresh air. I'll go for a run and pick up my car on the way round, killing two birds with one stone. I change into my running things, grab my keys and head out. Just as I'm locking the door behind me, I notice Darcy walking towards me. I roll my eyes thinking, great, she lives here too. She looks me up and down as if she's just scraped me off the bottom of her shoe, sniffs dismissively, doesn't speak and flounces past me. I glance back at her as I'm leaving the building, and see her enter the flat opposite to Alison's. Brilliant, we're neighbours. I giggle, wondering what the chances are of me borrowing a cup of sugar.

I leave the building, inhaling deeply, filling my lungs with the cold, crisp air. I love sunny but chilly days. I smile, seeing leaves falling from the trees, dancing and swirling around in the wind, a whirlpool of oranges, reds and golden browns. It reminds me of happier times – playing in the garden with my parents, chasing leaves as Dad raked them from the grass into piles, and when he'd finished we'd all jump into them, giggling and laughing. Dad would chase Mum and me around the garden, kicking the leaves high into the air while we ran to see how many we could catch. Afterwards we'd have a competition to see who could make the biggest pile of leaves. The winner got to sit on the heap and drink hot chocolate. Somehow, I was always the winner. I sigh heavily. Happy, happy times.

I start to run, heading towards the car park. As I pick up speed, taking in deep gulps of air, I feel vibrant and alive. The wind is blowing through my hair, and my cheeks feel cold as the frosty air nips at them.

A car goes passed me, and my mouth is practically open as I stare at it – an Aston Martin in my favourite colour, British racing green.

"Wow," I mutter out loud.

The driver pips his horn, but I don't notice; I'm far too busy ogling the car. I carry on running, heading towards the car park and praying that my little yellow car hasn't been towed. I spot it still on the grass verge where I left it. I glance up to the sky, saying, "Thank you, Lord!" But as I get closer I can see that it's actually in a shallow ditch. Looks like I spoke too soon. Great! How the hell am I going to get it out of there?

I reach my car opening the door, placing the key into the ignition, turning it. Nothing.

"Agh, you're not going to start, are you?"

I get out, cursing at the car like it can hear me, as if that will help. "Great, just bloody great!"

"Are you okay there, love?" I turn and see a good-looking man approaching me. Dark haired, in his late twenties. "Need some help?" he asks, looking me up and down.

"No, you'll get filthy." He's dressed in a very smart suit. "I'll be okay, but thank you for the offer anyway." I smile at the kind gesture.

"Nonsense," he says, holding out his hand. "I'm James."

"Abigail," I say back.

He gestures with his hand towards my car.

"Well, get in and I'll give you a push."

"Are you sure about this?"

"Yes, it's fine."

"Okay, well thank you, if you're sure."

I jump into my car and remove the handbrake.

"Ready?" I shout, and he starts to push.

It moves slightly forward, but then rolls back. My wheels spin and mud from my tyres sprays everywhere. I quickly jump out of the car to look, and I shouldn't, but I start to laugh. I try to stifle it, but James is covered in mud splats and he looks so funny. I suddenly realise that I'm being rude, and stop abruptly, startled by my behaviour.

"Oh dear, I'm sorry! That was really rude of me." I start to walk around to the back of the car, holding in my laughter. "But you do look funny. Let me see if I have a towel."

I open the boot but I only have baby wipes. I hand them to him.

"Will these do?" I say sheepishly.

"Thanks." He looks at the wipes, then his shirt and trousers, and rolls his eyes. He passes them back to me. "It's okay. I'll change inside. It was worth it to help a beautiful damsel in distress." He laughs. "So, do you work here? I've not seen you around before."

"I'm a student. I've just started," I answer politely.

"Which ward are you on?"

"ENT."

He moves closer to me, nodding his head and smiling. Then he takes me by surprise and suddenly starts brushing my hair away from my face, shaking his head.

"This looks nasty." He studies the dressing on my head, moving closer as he does so; he's almost touching my body with his.

I feel a little discomforted by his familiarity.

"Do you want me to take a look at that for you?" he says smoothly, moving his finger down the side of my cheek.

I step backwards, flummoxed, and reply flatly, "No, I'm fine, thank you." He's a little too forward for my liking.

His eyes have raised as I continue to edge away.

"So, I'll be seeing lots more of you while I'm on my rounds, will I?"

I smile uncomfortably.

"That's a beautiful smile you have." He winks at me. "Well, Abigail," he continues as he holds out his hand for me to shake. I take it to be polite, and to my horror he starts rubbing my wrist with his thumb. I don't know what to do. I try to pull my hand away, but he grips it tight and finishes his sentence. "It was lovely to meet you, and to help you out."

He continues to rub my wrist, making me feel even more awkward, but giving him a small smile, thinking, *Please let go.*

His eyes wander over me. "Can we meet for a drink sometime?"

I don't answer him and pull my hand free, knowing I need to cut this conversation dead before he starts up again.

"Thank you for helping me," I say nervously as I lock the

car, not wanting to encourage him further, although I know I've not said anything to encourage him to start with.

"Anytime. For you, anytime." His tone is still very suggestive, and he smirks as he raises his eyebrows at me.

He reminds me of Adam, and I just want to get out of there. He's watching my every move, making me feel on edge. He's forward, but not in a good way. I get a strange feeling in my stomach – something just doesn't sit right with him. I turn and start to run in the opposite direction, although I can feel him watching me. I have a funny, and not particularly pleasant, feeling about that man.

As I near the flat I see the same Aston Martin setting off from the roadside. I don't pay much attention to it as my mind is still on James. I feel as though I need to wash my hands. I run past building and continue on for another half hour, trying to run him out of my head. Then I turn round and head back to the flat.

I reach the car park and head inside. The coast is clear, and there are no friendly neighbours around. I open the door and go into the kitchen for a drink, then wash my hands as a shiver runs down my spine. I need to stop thinking about James, about the way he spoke to me and touched me. I don't know why I keep dwelling on him, but he gave me the creeps.

I go to my room and sit on the bed, getting my breath back. I check my phone, seeing more text messages and missed calls from the same private number. Once again, I don't read or listen to them. I know they're from Adam, and I don't want to start thinking about him either right now. I lie back on the bed, and, surprisingly, fall quickly asleep.

When I wake up it's dark outside and my tummy's rumbling. I wander into the kitchen and open the cupboards, looking for something to eat. I find a can of soup, warm it up, and sit eating it at the table with some bread and butter. I feel a little better now. I wash the dish and plate and run myself a bath. After, I sit in the lounge in my pyjamas, feet curled up on the sofa, watching the telly. It's late when Alison arrives home, but we watch some more telly together before we both go off to bed.

I'm curled up beneath the duvet but I can't seem to sleep. I keep thinking of Edward, knowing that I'll be seeing him on the ward tomorrow, and mulling over what Alison told me about Darcy, how she's infatuated with him. Then there's everything else she told me about him, and how he feels about me. I remember how I've behaved towards him, telling him to leave when all he did was care. Saying all those nasty things about him when he could hear me. I dread to think how he's going to react to me tomorrow.

Eventually I doze off.

The alarm wakes me at 6 a.m. This will be my first day on the ward as a student nurse, rather than a patient. I shake my head and grin apprehensively to myself. I have a bad feeling about today; I have to face Mr Bossy Pants and he's going to give me hell, that much I'm certain of. He was livid with me yesterday. I think I bruised his precious male ego. Can I blame him, though, for being angry? I wouldn't have been best pleased if I'd overheard someone talking about me like that. However, what's done is done. I can't take it back. I can apologise, and just maybe he'll forgive me. Huh! Forgive and forget? He doesn't seem like the forgiving type. I'm giving myself a headache wondering what he's going to say, and how he's going to react.

I make my way to the bathroom and start running the shower, being mindful not to get my head wet this time. Then I return to my room to find my uniform hung up, washed and ironed by Alison.

"Thank you," I shout as I dress.

"You're welcome," she shouts back.

We come out of our rooms and Alison threads her arm through mine. "Ready?"

"As I'll ever be!" I say, apprehensively, then shake my

head answering truthfully. "Actually, no, not really. I'm dreading this, but needs must when the devil drives." I chuckle at my own wit, and Alison groans good-humouredly.

"I don't think he's that bad," she replies hesitantly.

I cock my head to one side and simply reply, "Really?"

She doesn't answer, which in my mind confirms that she actually agrees with me, but is too polite to say so.

We arrive on the ward, put our bags away and make our way to the staff room for the handover. I sit quietly while Sister goes through the patients.

"We have a new doctor on the ward today," Sister says, as she finishes the handover. "He's covering for Mr Scott."

"Where's Mr Scott?" Darcy asks, puzzled.

"He's away for a few days."

"Where's he gone?"

"That is none of our business, is it?" Sister replies crossly.

Some of the nurses turn to look at me, although I'm just as surprised as everyone else. He never said he was going away, and I can't help but wonder where he's gone. Alison gives me a questioning look; I shrug my shoulders. Sister then informs me that Darcy is to be my mentor, then promptly leaves the handover. I'm going to have to take my orders from my worst nightmare, Miss Bitch of the Year. Nevertheless, I smile back at her, telling myself to hold it together. I remind myself of how much I want this job. I smile despondently at Alison, who gives me a sympathetic good-luck look in return. Darcy grins vindictively at me, then starts with the job list.

"Right, you can start in bay one. You'll need to assist all the patients who need help with washing and dressing. Then make all the beds. When you've finished that, you can clean the bed frames underneath with hot soapy water. Every bed in bay one needs to be cleaned properly. I will check, and if they're not done right, I'll fail you on the simplest of nursing skills, okay?"

I know what I want to say to her: *Anything else while you're on a roll? Maybe I can stick a broom up my arse and sweep the floor?* Some of the other nurses snigger. Darcy grins with satisfaction, knowing that I don't have any choice but to do what she says.

I suck in my pride and reply, "That's fine, no problem. Would you like me to start straight away?" I smile very sweetly at her, and she just glares back. Being over-nice to her has pissed her off, and she doesn't bother replying.

I enter bay one with a smile.

"Good morning!" I say cheerfully, trying my best to sound professional. "I'm a student nurse, and my name is Abigail."

I walk confidently over to the first bed, but inside I'm terrified. I introduce myself again and say, "Good morning, Mr Leaver."

He nods his head at me and winks. He's a thirty-year-old male, admitted to hospital with continuous heavy nosebleeds, the medical term for which is acute epistaxis. Both nostrils were cauterised, although this didn't stop the bleeding. He's since had his nose packed. Sister informed us that he needs to be monitored regularly for hypertension, a possible cause of the nosebleeds, and that any bleeding should be recorded. I'm not monitoring his blood pressure or recording any bleeding, as Darcy has very kindly pointed out to me that this is "down to the trained staff, as they know exactly what they're doing". Oh, and didn't she just love making that comment – she said it with such an air of satisfaction. I'm trying my best not to stare at Mr Leaver's nose. He has packs up each nostril and the strings are hanging down onto his face, as if he has a couple of tampons in his nose. I'm trying hard not to laugh.

"Would you like any help?" I ask him in a croaky voice

He grins. "What have you got in mind, love?"

I raise my eyebrows and speak firmly, as if I know what I'm doing.

"Help with washing and dressing."

"Oh, that would be very nice," he replies with a smirk.

A man shouts from bed three.

"I wouldn't mind some help, love!"

Another patient shouts, "Well, if you're offering then I'll have some of that too."

I start blushing, and I'm silently furious with myself. *Abbie, how stupid are you? Darcy's well and truly set me up, and I fell for it. The cow!* The entire bay is now in an uproar; all the men are laughing and shouting, joking with each other at my expense. I cringe as Sister strides into the bay, her face set in a scowl.

"What is going on in here? Nurse Baxter, why is there all this shouting?"

"Bloody hell! If she's helping you then I'd rather not bother. I'm not having her washing my crown jewels," Mr Leaver shouts.

My eyes are like saucers. Oh God, she must be fuming.

"That will do, Mr Leaver."

He pulls a face at me.

"Nurse Baxter, see me in my office. Immediately, please." I follow her into the room. She looks furious and shakes her head at me. I desperately want to shut my eyes, and I literally have to stop myself from shaking. God, this woman terrifies me, and all I ever seem to do when she's around is mess everything up.

"Is it your intention to upset the ward every time you enter it, Nurse Baxter?" she bellows. I can't speak. I feel as though I'm about five years old. "Well, answer me! Is it?"

"No, Sister," I reply quietly, hoping she'll take pity on me. Who am I kidding? Her face is practically scarlet. "Sorry, Sister," I say meekly, but it doesn't work and she continues to rant on.

"Humph! Then use some intelligence. Those are young men out there. I don't really think they need any help with washing or dressing, do you? And they certainly don't need any encouragement from the female staff."

"I'm sorry. It won't happen again," I say despondently.

"Yes, well, make sure it doesn't, or you will be off this ward quicker than you can blink. Do I make myself clear?"

Her stare is aloof; does she want me to reply? Oh, Lord, I don't know what to do. Should I tell her that Darcy's setting me up? Or is that too much like telling tales? I'm suddenly reminded of what Edward said to me about being childish, so I decide not to say anything. Instead, I take the brunt of it and wait to be dismissed.

I leave Sister's office, annoyed and slightly disappointed that once again I didn't stand up for myself. I'm simmering away like a witch's cauldron, just waiting to boil and then erupt. I wish that I was a witch; then I'd put a spell on them both. I see Darcy laughing as she waits by bay one. I'm sure she was listening. No, I know darned well she was. I smile sweetly, although my first reaction is to scream in her face. It's tempting, but why should I lower myself to her level? So instead I smile at her, and that stops her laughing. She looks uncertain now as I walk up to her. Revenge is a dish best served cold, I think, trying to keep calm.

"I'll continue with bay one, shall I? Now that little misunderstanding's been cleared up, thanks to Sister's wonderful advice." I can tell by the look on her face that she's wondering what's been said. I walk past her and re-enter the bay.

"Sorry," Mr Leaver says with a sheepish smile.

I shake my head and smile at him, getting on with the task ahead. Before long, I've finished the bay, and it sparkles like a new pin. My hands feel like sandpaper from all the scrubbing and cleaning, but I've done a good job. I didn't want to give Darcy the satisfaction of saying I couldn't do it right.

Alison pops her head in. "Hi, Abbie. Are you having a break?"

I shake my head at her. "No, I don't think so. I've probably got more jobs to do, and when I've finished in here I've to go and find Darcy to tell her I'm done."

She rolls her eyes at me. "Chin up, Abbie! See you at the

end of the shift then, and I'll make you some lunch."

"Thanks, but I'm fine. She doesn't faze me in the least. I've dealt with worse than her in my time, trust me. Go and get your break. I'll see you later."

I find Darcy and tell her I've finished, and she gives me more jobs to do. I carry on with these until the end of my shift. Alison comes to find me and says that Sister has said we can go. I get my things from the staff room, but as we're leaving the ward Darcy starts yelling at me.

"Did I say you could leave?"

I shake my head at her.

"No, but Sister told me I could go."

I smile smugly, and she looks annoyed. I shrug my shoulders. She's about to say something else when she spots something over my shoulder.

"Oh, hi!" she says flirtatiously, and I wonder for a second if she's seen Edward. "You must be Dr Bailey." She's blushes coyly and holds her hand out.

I turn, horrified to see that it's James. I guess that's what he meant when he said he'd see lots more of me. An unpleasant lurch is triggered in my stomach. He takes Darcy's hand, shaking it while looking at me and smiling with that creepy leer of his.

"Abigail."

I cringe at the way he says my name, lingering on it. "Nice to see you again. Are you keeping well? Have you managed to get your car started yet? And have you thought about that drink?"

I shake my head and shudder. Alison and Darcy both look at me in surprise, and it's no wonder after the suggestive way he's just spoken. He's implied that we know each other well. He makes my bones creak, and I'm so desperate to leave and not get into a conversation with him.

"I'm sorry, I need to dash," I reply flatly, grabbing Alison's arm. "Come on or we'll miss the bus."

Thankfully she plays along. I can hear Darcy talking to

him as we leave.

"Dr Bailey, I'll show you round the ward if you like. I'm the deputy sister, and if you want me to give you a tour any time after work then I'd be pleased to walk you round the hospital and grounds."

My eyes widen at her forwardness. There's no flies on her, as my gran would say.

I don't hear his reply, but they walk off together, chatting like old friends. I'm hoping he takes the hint that I'm not interested in him in the slightest.

"What was all that about?" Alison asks as we're leaving the ward.

I tell her about meeting him while I was out running, and what happened with my car.

Alison pulls a face. "Ugh! Creepy."

I nod in agreement. "Yes, tell me about it!"

Chapter 11

Another day back on the wards and, for me, today is a long shift. Alison's on the late shift so she's still in bed, sleeping. I wish I was too because I'm shattered. I didn't get much sleep again last night. I have thirteen hours to work today, and no doubt Darcy will be on my back again.

Alison asked Tom if he knew where Edward had gone, but he didn't. He said he hadn't heard from him, although someone mentioned that he'll be coming back on Monday. It all seems a bit of a mystery as to where he's gone, especially at such short notice, but I think Edward is a bit ... well, a huge mystery, full stop. I don't know where I am with him; one minute he's here and wanting to see me, the next, *poof*, he's gone, just like that. No explanation, no phone call, no nothing.

I'm trying to stay positive about everything that's happening in my life. Everything's changing, I think, as I tiptoe about, getting ready and trying not to wake Alison. I put on my uniform, tie my hair up, grab my paperwork and leave the flat, eating a banana as I go. Darcy is ahead of me in the corridor, but she's not wearing her uniform. I punch the air with delight. Yes! She's not working today.

I follow her out silently. She turns and smirks at me as she climbs into James's car. They're out and about early, and it's only 7.20 a.m. Then I chuckle to myself. As if I give a damn! God, she is so welcome to him. In fact, I think they make a lovely couple. They're both deranged, and maybe he'll leave me alone now. As for Darcy, if she's finally bagged herself a doctor then maybe she'll back off too.

I walk to the ward a little more uplifted, knowing that the psycho is out with the letch and I don't have to see them all day. Maybe today will be a good day after all.

I arrive on the ward and sit in the staff room, waiting for

the handover from Sister.

When she's finished, she asks me to wait in the room until everyone leaves. I'm a little puzzled as to why. Perhaps I'm going to be told off for something that I have, or haven't, done.

"Abigail, you'll be working with me today," she says. "I'm going to start going through your paperwork with you at some point later."

I want to roll my eyes at her, but I smile instead, nodding my head and thinking that maybe it won't be a good day after all.

"I've also got a message for you."

My heart jumps, and I can feel my face flushing.

"I had a telephone call earlier."

I smile to myself, wondering if the message is from Edward.

"From your husband." My face drops visibly, which she can't help but notice. "He asked for your address and what shifts you're working."

My eyes grow wide and my heart picks up speed. Why can't he just leave me alone?

"You didn't tell him, did you?" I blurt.

She shakes her head and smiles slightly, and I realise that she knows I'm scared. "He's not a nice person, is he?"

I shake my head mutely.

"No need to explain," she continues kindly. "And, no, I didn't give him your address or tell him about your shifts."

"Thank you," I say breathily. "And the message?"

"I'm sorry," she sighs, "but I suppose you do need to know. Do you want me to tell you what he said? Word for word?"

I nod reluctantly.

"Well, his exact words were, 'Tell the little bitch to answer my calls and reply to my messages. She'd be a fool to ignore me. I know which ward she works on.' And then he slammed the phone down."

"Oh God!" I moan softly. I put my hands to my face, closing my eyes to hide my emotions, but what I really want to do is stamp my feet and scream. This is because he's not getting his own way any more. Threats, mind games, all over again. Will he ever stop, or understand he can't keep doing this to me? Sister puts her hand on my shoulder, making me jump.

"I'm sorry," she says, seeing how scared I am. "Are you okay?"

I move my hands from my face and open my eyes.

"I will be. Thank you." I let out a deep sigh.

"We have very good security here at the hospital, if you need to use them."

I smile at her concern. Alison was right; she's not that bad after all. Well, as long as I'm not disrupting her ward, that is.

Her voice is sympathetic now. "You take five minutes, and then come and find me."

She leaves me on my own in the room. I'm so afraid that my hands are trembling. I hate him. He's a bully and I wish to God that he would leave me alone, but I know he never will. He's always done this to me, made me feel weak, so he could control me. He doesn't like it because I've stuck up for myself, and I'm not answering his calls or text messages. He's resorted to playing mind games again because he can't hit me. I'm no longer there to be his punch bag. But him ringing the ward, saying what he did to Sister? This is new, him giving away some part of his precious reputation like that, and to a total stranger. I sigh deeply with concern, wondering what he's playing at.

I feel like I don't really know myself any more, but after four years with Adam, is it any wonder? I'm trying to break free and stop this chain of unhappy events, but it feels like every time I get over one hurdle I'm faced with another, twice the size. I don't know if I can carry on like this. One minute I'm happy, trying my hardest to get back on track, and the next I'm confused, scared and mixed up. My mood is once again at rock bottom. I feel strange, lonely and despondent. I try to convince myself to move on once and for all as I take a deep breath, put on a brave face with my false smile, and go to find Sister.

She gives me a list of jobs to do. I'm working on my own for the best part of the morning, and I wonder whether she's planned it that way. I'm glad of it, though, as I don't feel like talking much, or having to listen to idle gossip about where Edward is or, more importantly, who he's with.

I shake my head at some of the staff talking in the corridor as I walk past them towards the sluice room with a bedpan. I listen to them complaining about how they forgot to put the bin out, and how they can't remember if they fed the cat before they left for work. They think they have problems? I'd love to swap theirs for mine, even for just one day.

I roll my eyes as I leave the sluice room and walk up the corridor towards the nurses' station to find Sister. As I'm passing one of the private side rooms, a patient waves at me from her bed. I'm a little scared of entering at first, as I don't know what she wants, but I can't ignore the fact that she's crying, so I go in. I smile, noticing her nurse-call is out of reach on the floor. I bend to pick it up.

"Do you need some help?" I ask. She nods at me through her tears. "Okay, tell me what you want."

I look above her bed to find her name as I've not had any dealings with the patients in the private side rooms. *Mrs Baker.* And underneath her name, *Con: Mr Scott.*

She's the laryngectomy patient I heard about on my first day, before I had my accident. I didn't see that when I first entered her room. She can't speak at all, and I cringe at my insensitivity. *Tell me what you want.*

She's still crying but she smiles slightly, picking up her pen and pad from the table. I look nervously at her neck. The laryngectomy wound looks inflamed and sore. How did I not notice that? I want to kick myself, because I was too busy feeling nervous and worrying about my own problems, thinking about myself instead of these poor patients. I feel so selfish.

The other staff have their small problems, and I have mine with Adam, but reality has just hit me like a freight train. My problems are nothing compared to this woman's. One of the things we take for granted in life is the ability to speak, to communicate with each other. It's part of what makes us human. But that's been taken away from her. She's scared and embarrassed.

She starts to write: "I'm sorry. I've had a little accident and I'm so embarrassed. I dropped the nurse-call on the floor, and I couldn't shout for help. I was too scared to go to the bathroom on my own, as I feel a little dizzy."

I study her face, feeling so sorry for her, knowing it must be awful not being able to talk or ask for what you need.

"Do you want me to help you to the bathroom? I'll sort out your bed while you're in there."

She nods gratefully and we make our way there.

Her nightdress is wet.

"I'll help you change it," I say, and I walk back to her room, open the drawer and taking out her toiletry bag. I find a clean nightdress and some underwear, then return to the bathroom to help her wash and change.

I can't take my eyes off her neck, and the noise that she makes when she breathes is very distracting. It looks so sore.

"I'll just do your bed for you, Mrs Baker." She smiles in response.

I return to her room, strip the bed, take the wet bedding to the slice room, then go to the laundry cupboard to get clean sheets. As I'm returning, Sister stops me.

"Who are those sheets for?"

"Mrs Baker."

"Mrs Baker?" she asks puzzled.

"Yes, I'm just changing her bed. She spilt her water," I add. There are a few people passing, and I don't want Mrs Baker to feel any more embarrassed than she already does by having everybody know what's happened.

"Her water?" Sister still looks puzzled, and it dawns on me that a laryngectomy patient wouldn't be able to drink water. I nod all the same, hoping she doesn't ask me any further questions. She raises an eyebrow at me, but lets it go. "Carry on then," she says, walking away.

I return to Mrs Baker's room, make her bed and help her back into it. She starts to cough and looks at me, panicked. She coughs harder; mucus mixed with blood starts to come from the hole in her neck. It looks like it might be blocked. She grabs my hand, looking terrified. I hit the emergency-call bell and Sister flies into the room, taking in the situation at a glance. I'm petrified for Mrs Baker as she can't breathe. Sister grabs the suction from the wall, as I quickly move out of her way. I'm shaking. I've never seen anything like this, nor thought I ever would. I don't know what to do and feel so helpless. I just stand there as Sister suctions the hole in her neck with the tube. Two other nurses come running in and Sister barks orders at them.

"It's okay, the emergency's over with."

Mrs Baker breathes normally again, or as normally as she can. "Mrs Baker, is that better?" Sister asks gently, patting her hand.

She nods in response, and starts to calm down, but I still feel anxious. I don't think I'll ever be able to do what Sister has just done. She was so calm, knowing exactly what to do. My tummy is turning over and my hands are still shaking.

"Abigail, please stay with Mrs Baker until she's settled. Is that okay with you, Mrs Baker?"

She nods, and Sister leaves the room.

Mrs Baker starts to write "Thank you, Abigail." She's thanking me for what I did for her, but I did nothing. Sister did everything. I don't know what to say to her. I study her for a moment. She's about forty-five, and is wearing a wedding ring. I smile at her as she leans towards her drawers and takes out her purse. She pulls a photo out. A tear trickles down her cheek as she points to the picture, and I squeeze her hand in empathy.

The photo shows her before the operation, with her husband and two young children. Her family. They all look very happy together. She looks so young, and you can tell from the way they're looking at her that they adore her.

"They're beautiful," I say, holding back my tears. "What are they called?"

She gets her pad, smiling. "Rosie; she's five and very cheeky …" I smile. "And Andrew is six, and very lively."

"I would love to meet them when they visit," I say.

She gives me the biggest smile, and you can tell that they're her whole world.

"Are you married? Do you have any children?" she writes. I shake my head to both, although only the latter is true. "What, a beautiful looking girl like you?"

I smile shyly, and she continues. "I'm hoping Mr Scott will discharge me, although he's very strict and said I was only able to go home if everything is in place and I was confident in looking after the stoma site myself" She smiles, and continues writing. "He's a lovely man, and very handsome, but don't tell my husband I …" She stops writing, and I know what she's thinking. *Don't tell my husband I said that.* But she didn't say it, she wrote it.

I feel so sorry for her. Her children will never hear their mummy's voice again. She seems like such a lovely person and doesn't deserve this. I smile sadly at her.

"I'd better go and find Sister. Are you okay with that? If your children visit then I'd love to meet them, but I'm off tomorrow, and not back on the ward until Thursday next week."

"I'll look forward to it, if I'm still here," she writes.

"Me too, Mrs Baker. I'll see you later."

She waves at me as I leave her room. I feel like I want to cry, although I'm not sure why any more. My situation, or maybe hers; the way I panicked when she started choking.

Meeting her has certainly put my own life into perspective all of a sudden – I'm certain of that.

I think that perhaps Joe was right when he told me that by helping other people, then maybe I could help myself. I need to tell him that I've started at the hospital. He gave me the courage to do this, to become a student nurse, and he made me realise what Adam was really like. I already knew, deep down, but hearing it from someone else makes you sit up and listen.

I go to find Sister, and she smiles warmly at me.

"That was a good job you did with Mrs Baker. Well done. Now let's go to my office and start your paperwork."

I'm taken aback because I don't really feel that I've done anything.

We start on the paperwork and complete half of it by lunchtime.

Then sister tells me to go to the library on my break to get some books and to start revising for my presentation, which is due after Christmas.

I make my way through the hospital grounds. I'm hoping the fresh air will clear my head. I grab a sandwich and apple from the shop on the way.

By the time I reach the library, my head is spinning with the events of the morning: Adam and his nasty message, Mrs Baker and, of course, Edward. He never seems to leave my thoughts, and he's the main cause of my confusion and headache.

I fill out my application to join, and the librarian gives me a card. I'm browsing through the section on ENT when a name catches my eye. I smile, shaking my head. Everywhere I go in the hospital, everywhere I look, I'm reminded of Edward. His name is everywhere. It seems like the universe isn't going to let me forget him. It's fate, my gran would say. I recall Mrs Baker's words: *He's a lovely man, and very handsome.* I think someone is in cahoots with my subconscious, but I don't know who!

Head and Neck Surgery by Edward Scott. *Throat Cancer* by Edward Scott. *Laryngeal Cancer* by Edward Scott. *Tracheostomy Care* by Edward Scott. The list goes on. Wow. He's very clever, and has a lot of books published.

I remember what Alison said to me, that Edward told Tom he likes me. Why me? He's got everything, and I'd be way out of my depth with him. What on earth would we have in common? He's an accomplished writer, a top surgeon, at the peak of his game. Handsome, bossy, arrogant. I laugh to myself, because the list goes on and on.

However, curiosity gets the better of me and I check out two of his books. Maybe these will give me an insight into the real Mr Edward Scott.

I make my way back to the ward and sit in the staff room on my own, eating my sandwich. I reach for my bag and take out one of Edward's books. There's a dedication on the first page that makes me smile:

To my mother and father, to whom I owe everything.

It's beautiful; what a nice thing to say. I would never have guessed that he could be so sentimental or caring. Do I add that to the list of his personal attributes now? Then again, he probably likes his parents, and, contrary to what Tom says, I still don't think he likes me. He's certainly an enigma, though, just one surprise after another.

I sit back, turn to the first chapter and start to read as I eat my sandwich. After a few paragraphs, I shake my head. I have no idea at all what I'm reading. I can't even pronounce some of the words. I try my best to carry on, but I'm completely baffled.

Suspension micro-laryngoscopy, the laser refined direct laryngoscopy, and excisional biopsy. Hemi-laryngectomy and vertical partial laryngectomy succeeded laryngofissure and cordectomy. Supraglottic laryngectomy conserved voice and nasal breathing for patients formerly consigned to total laryngectomy.

I'm nearly cross-eyed! Hell, if I have to understand any of

that to become a nurse then I might as well leave now.

I check the time, put the book back into my bag and go to find Sister.

She asks if I've been to the library, and I nod. It's hard to be sure with her, but I think she's pleased with me.

"What books did you check out?"

I smile sheepishly at her.

"Umm, I can't remember what they were called." I'm embarrassed, and don't want to admit I checked out Edward's books.

"Oh, well, never mind. You can show me when we finish off your paperwork later."

I nod, but think, *God, nothing gets past her.*

We work together, and she works me hard. I've enjoyed myself today, although I have a headache. I've learnt loads, and she's even let me loose on some patients. I did okay, apart from pumping up the cuff on the blood-pressure machine a little too high on my first patient because he kept talking to me and moving about. I was struggling to hear the sounds of the beat as it came in, then out, but Sister insisted I use the manual sphygmomanometer with cuff and stethoscope and not the new digital machine. He survived, although he was a little bruised after my sixth attempt, but I told him politely that it was quite a tricky procedure. He smiled courteously at me, saying it wasn't a problem, and that everyone has to learn. Then he raised an eyebrow at Sister, who thanked him for his patience as we left.

She showed me how to write the patients' blood pressures on the graphs, explained what the normal ranges were, and what to do if it was abnormal. I've taken patients' temperatures, SpO2 readings and samples, filled in the cards and delivered them to the path lab. I actually feel like a student nurse today.

I had my tea break with Alison, and over our drinks I told her about Adam ringing the ward, and the message he left with Sister. She looked worried, and offered to chaperone me everywhere I go. I didn't tell her about Mrs Baker, as I thought that would be gossiping about her, but I did tell her about the books I got out from the library, and she raised her eyebrows at me. She roared when I told her about the six attempts it took me to take my patient's blood pressure and the bruising I left behind, and I found myself thinking again that I really like Alison, and how nice it is to have a friend. We agreed to meet in the staff room after our shifts and walk home together. In fact, Alison had insisted, because of Adam.

After my tea break, I continue to work with Sister; then we go to her office around 7.30 p.m. to finish off my paperwork.

"Show me the books you got from the library today."

I was hoping she'd forgotten about that.

I go to get my bag from the staff room, feeling embarrassed and hoping she's not going to test me on them, because I know I'll fail miserably. I return to her office and take the books out of my bag. She smirks at me as I put them on the table. I feel stupid, and my face starts to flush. I feel like a schoolgirl in the headmistress's office again. Sister gestures with her hand for me to sit down as she picks up one of the books and studies the front cover.

"How did you find them? I presume you've already started to read them."

I nod and go bright red, but I need to be honest with her.

"They were very hard going, if I'm being honest with you. Some of the words I couldn't even read. I didn't really understand any of it."

She sits back in her chair, watching me silently, and I wonder if she thinks that I'm a disaster. She finally speaks.

"So you're going to be a surgeon, and not a nurse?" I look confused. I don't understand what she means – a surgeon, not a nurse? "Maybe be you didn't understand them because you were in the wrong section of the library. Although I appreciate your honesty. Was it the author's name that attracted you to the books, by any chance?"

My face flushes even brighter now, and I know I'm busted. I did get them because Edward wrote them, and then it dawns on me – he's a surgeon; of course he'd write books for surgeons, not student nurses. *Duh, Abbie.*

She smiles at me as she sees the penny drop. She writes some book titles down on a piece of paper and hands it to me with a chuckle.

"Try these. I'm sure they'll be more suitable for your poster presentation."

"Thank you. I feel a little silly."

"Not at all." I'm sure she's trying not to laugh at me. "It's an easy mistake to make, I'm sure. But may I suggest you ask the librarian to give you a tour next time, so you know which section is more suitable for your career." Then she raises her eyebrows at me.

"Yes, I'll do that. Thank you."

I work with Sister for the rest of the shift, then meet Alison in the staff room as arranged. We walk home together, talking about our day. We're both shattered, and my brain hurts. It's been overworked today, what with everything that has happened. We both say goodnight to each other and make our way to our rooms for a well-earned early night.

Chapter 12

Alison and I are off today. I'm still in bed, having a well-deserved lie-in. I'm just stretching out my arms and legs when Alison taps at my door, opening it slightly.

"Come in," I say, as she pops her head through the door.

"Morning. I've made breakfast if you'd like some."

I nod. "Umm, please. It smells good," I say as the sweet smell of porridge and honey wafts into my room. I throw the duvet back and lazily get out of bed, yawning and stretching. "I'll just use the bathroom first."

"Yeah, no worries. I'll get the coffee." She smiles and leaves my room. I follow behind her, making my way to the bathroom. I use the loo, wash my hands and face and return to the lounge to find Alison sitting at the table. I'm puzzled – there's a coffee pot, hot croissants, jams and three bowls, three cups and three plates. She moves her eyes upwards silently as she notices my face. "Tom was coming, but he's just called to say he has to go into work."

"Oh, did you have plans?" I say, quite genuinely gutted for her as I see the flash of disappointment over her face.

"Well, yes, but that's doctors for you, Abbie." She chews her lip and stares at me. I just shake my head, knowing she's tip-toeing around the mention of Edward.

"Please don't act any differently on my behalf about Tom. I'm fine, honestly." She smiles and we say no more about it.

We sit and eat our breakfast, which is extremely good. I hadn't realised how hungry I was. We're having a second coffee when Alison asks a question.

"Do you fancy coming to the club tonight? There's a band on. Tom said they're really good, and it might cheer you up." She nods her head for me to say yes, and I smile inwardly. She really does think I'm sad, and she's still nodding trying to persuade me to say yes.

"Okay, but only if you let me buy you dinner."

"Great! it will be so much fun," she replies with a beaming smile, and I can't help but smile back.

"Is Tom going?" I ask.

"Yes, but not until later. Is that okay?"

"Of course it is. Anyway, I've no one to take, and I haven't been out in ages. I'm really looking forward to it now."

"What are you up to today?"

I'm glad she's asked.

"I was going to suggest that I'd make a Sunday roast for you and Tom tomorrow, if you're both free. As a way of saying thank you for letting me stay, and a sort of apology for all the other stuff." I frown. "You know …"

"You don't need to do that! I love having you here. You're like the sister I never had."

"Ditto, but I'd like to do this for you, so please let me. I'll go to the supermarket today and get everything I need. I've nothing else to do."

"Okay. Thank you!"

"What are you doing today?"

"I'm still going to see my dad. He's had another argument with my mum," she says as she goes to her room to get ready.

I'm washing up in the kitchen when Alison pops her head through the doorway.

"You don't have to clean up, Abbie."

"It's fine," I say with a smile. "I don't mind, really."

"Thanks. I'm off now. I'll be back around five. You have a good day."

"You too, and I hope all goes well with your dad."

"So do I. I feel like banging their heads together sometimes."

I finish up in the kitchen and tidy around the flat. I wash and dress, then head off to the local supermarket.

By the time I arrive, I know exactly what I want to cook for Alison and Tom – roast beef and Yorkshire puddings with all the trimmings. I've not made that since I was living at my gran's. Adam and I never sat down to meals together because he usually went to his mum's on a Sunday, and then the pub, while I had to stay in the house doing the chores, ready for work on Monday. I inhale deeply, knowing how stupid I've been for not insisting on having a life of my own all these years.

I stroll around the aisles, smiling and enjoying the unaccustomed freedom, knowing I don't have to worry about getting home before Adam. If I was out and he arrived home before me, he'd question me as to where I'd been, even though it was pretty obvious from all my shopping bags. He would still rant and rave, wanting to control every minute of my life. Sundays, he went to his mum's, and stayed there all day. I didn't have to endure that, thank God, as she wanted to spend time with her precious son on her own. And she was bloody welcome to him, although it never stopped him from ringing the house phone constantly, to make sure I was there and that I'd not sneaked out.

Wednesday was my only reprieve from him; it was the only time he allowed me to spend with my gran, but I knew why – he didn't want her becoming suspicious of his controlling ways. He'd finish work early every Wednesday, come home, shower, change and go out. He'd stay out till the early hours of the morning. I never asked where he went, and I didn't care, because it was the only day I looked forward to, more than anything in the world. He'd not hit me on Tuesdays either, or make me take part in his perverted, sick games in the bedroom. He was clever and sly, because the bruises and red marks he'd make would be fresh and visible on Wednesdays, and he couldn't risk my Gran seeing them. I recall what Joe said to me:

"For God's sake, Abbie, leave the sick bastard before he kills you."

Not that I'd ever told Joe that he was sadistic, that he liked it rough and hard, to tie me up and beat me until I cried, because that's what turned him on. I didn't need to tell him, he'd already guessed when he'd seen the red marks on my wrist and the fading hand print on my neck.

"Abbie," he'd said, "I thought you were just a little bit clumsy when I noticed the bruises, but there's a lot more to it than that, isn't there?"

I'd just shrugged my shoulders, knowing I couldn't explain that one. We talked, but Joe never pried. He let me speak when I felt I was able to. He helped me, and made me realise that Adam was a monster, that I should leave him before things really got out of hand. He said he knew what he was talking about, because when he'd been mixed up about his sexuality, he'd had a few abusive relationships himself.

We would call our meetings at the running club our therapy sessions. We helped each other. Joe was in his final few months before becoming a registrar at the hospital, and as time went on he talked me into becoming a student nurse. He's in a good place now – he's met someone really nice – but to look at him or hear him speak you would never guess that he was gay. He could have knocked me down with a feather when he told me. It made me think that life's never fair, because he was exactly the type of man you'd want to spend time with. He was kind, honest, loving, and so funny. Of course, he was also goddamn gorgeous.

He didn't like people knowing he was gay. There was still a lot of stigma attached to it, especially around the hospital. He'd said it was hard enough proving yourself, without any of your personal life cropping up and adding to the mix. The competition for jobs was fierce enough at qualifying time as it was. I promised him I'd never say anything to anyone. Although I told him that I knew he'd get a job and be wonderful at it. After all, the role he'd be taking was apt – a heart registrar. He'd looked confused, so I explained it to him – that it suited him down to the ground because he has a wonderful, kind heart.

He just laughed at me, knocked my shoulder, and then set off at a sprint.

After our chats, he'd shout, "Come on! Last one back has to buy the coffee."

Which, of course, was always me, as he had the physique of a triathlete. He also cheated, and set off first every time. He'd run back to me laughing, saying that he'd give me a chance, but we both knew that he could run backwards around the course and still beat me.

I chuckle to myself as I remember that, in the five months I was there, Joe never bought the coffee. I suddenly realise that I'm laughing out loud, and a few people are staring strangely at me. I stop abruptly, but give them a smile anyway.

I pick up the beef and the trimmings, and decide to make my gran's homemade scones. I wrinkle my nose up thinking about her. She taught me how to make them when I was a little girl. I used to love cooking and baking with her, but I've not done this for years. I grab some fruit, and a new water bottle. I wander down past the wine aisle, then double back, thinking it would be nice to have wine with the meal. I start scouring the shelves, confused by the thousands of bottles from all over the world. I see a member of staff and walk towards her, hoping for some advice. She turns around, but she doesn't look very happy, although her name badge reads, *Sandra. Happy to help.* I don't bother to ask her, thinking that perhaps she's having a bad day. I can certainly sympathise with that. To be on the safe side, knowing little or nothing about wine, I choose the wine my gran drinks.

I also pick up a large box of chocolates and a bouquet of flowers for Alison. I go through the checkout and pay. I've bought a lot more than I was going to, so I decide to get a taxi back to the flat.

The taxi pulls up in the car park outside the building. I pay my fare and remove the heavy shopping bags and flowers. I'm at the door, juggling them and trying to enter the key code, when it suddenly opens. It knocks me a little off balance, and an arm grabs me. I look to see who it is. James. I roll my eyes. Great, just what I need.

"Whoa! Hello there again, Abigail." He smiles that slimy leer and lingers too long on my name. "We're going to have to stop meeting like this, or people will start talking. Let me help you with your bags."

I'm about to say no, but it's too late. As he takes the last bag from me, he leaves his fingers on my hand a little too long, smiling creepily at me. It makes me shudder. I try not to make eye contact with him. He's so smarmy, and he gives me the heebie-jeebies. I presume that he's just come from Darcy's flat and is about to leave the building. I practically run up the corridor as he makes suggestive remarks behind me, his breathing weird and heavy. He keeps hold of my bags at my door as I get my keys out. I'm cringing inwardly. Oh no, does he think he's coming in?

He's still staring at me, his eyebrows raised as he undresses me with his eyes. They remind me of Adam's, but his are brown, dark bottomless pits, almost black, and his eyebrows meet in the middle, which is always a warning sign. I'm going to have to work on my naivety, because at first I'd thought he was attractive and helpful, but now that I know him, I see that this couldn't be further from the truth. Just like Adam in many ways.

He opens his mouth and speaks.

"I'd love a coffee, or a cold drink …" His voice is suggestive. "I've just worked up a thirst." He grins as his eyes flick towards Darcy's door. I nearly drop my keys on the floor. Oh my God, I cannot believe he's just said that. I'm going to have to be blunt, rude even, to get him off my back.

Suddenly, Darcy's door opens and I turn to look at her. She looks furious, and scowls at me. Her hair is messed up, and she's wearing a dressing gown with, I'm guessing, nothing else underneath. It's pretty obvious what's been going on. I want to be sick. Her tone is sharp and snappy as she sees James with my bags.

"James, what are you doing with her? I thought you were leaving."

145

"What does it look like I'm doing?" he bites back harshly.

She's taken aback, and I just want to get inside the flat. I open the door.

"You can leave the bags there, thanks."

He puts them down, and Darcy glares at us both. I grab them quickly and nearly run into the flat. I slam the door behind me, then lock it.

I can hear James shouting, "Just because I've fucked you, it doesn't mean you own me!"

"Sorry, I thought ..." She stops talking, but he continues to shout at her.

"Got it? Don't you ever do that again!"

"Will I see you tonight?" she asks quietly. "Please, I'm sorry. I'll not do it again, I promise."

"Maybe."

I hear him snap, and he walks off down the corridor. He really does remind me of Adam. Then I hear her door slam. Oh my Lord, I can't believe what I've just heard. After what he just said to her, is she mad, asking to see him later? Then I remember: that what I was like with Adam. I just didn't see it until it was too late, and then I was stuck. I should warn her, but someone like her wouldn't pay any attention to what I have to say. She'd probably think I wanted him for myself. I shudder at the thought. She must be so desperate to bag a doctor at any expense. After overhearing that conversation, I decide there and then to stay well away from them both.

I put the shopping away, make some coffee and decide to ring my gran. Our weekend together had been put on hold, as gran had to go and visit her brother, my Uncle Patrick, who'd sprained his ankle.

We chat for about twenty minutes about this and that, and it's nice to be able to talk freely with her without looking over my shoulder to see if Adam's there. She's happy that I'm going out that evening with Alison, and even more so when I tell her that I'm going to make her scones, although I think we both knew they won't be as good as hers.

She also notices that I sound happier than when we last spoke. She asks how my training's going, so I tell her a little of what I've been doing. I don't tell her about the mistakes I made. I say that I'm able to meet her next week for our usual Wednesday get-together in town, and promise her I'll bring Alison along with me; Gran wants to thank her personally for looking after me. I tell her there's no need, but she insists. I don't argue with her; I never do, not with my gran. In fact, I don't think we've ever had a wrong word between us. That's not to say we always see eye to eye on everything. Disagreements, she'd call them – and they were all about Adam.

Eventually we say goodbye.

I run a bath, and as I'm having a long soak in the hot water, I hear Alison come in, shouting to me.

"Abbie?"

"I'm in the bath."

"Okay. When you come out, I've something to tell you!"

I get out, dry myself off and put on my dressing gown. Then I make my way into the lounge where Alison is waiting for me. She wriggles about in her chair, impatient to share her news with me.

"You'll never guess what I heard from Tom today."

"What?"

"Dr Bailey is seeing Darcy! Well, according to Tom, he's seeing what he can get from her, if you know what I mean. Tom heard him bragging about it in the changing rooms."

"Really? Bragging. Urgh!"

"That's what I thought. How creepy."

I tell her about what happened when I returned from the supermarket, and what James had said to Darcy.

"I actually felt a little bit sorry for her," I concluded. "Although I don't know why, since she's such an utter cow."

"Does she never learn? But I should warn you, Abbie, he was talking about you as well."

"What?" I pull a face.

"Tom said he was saying that he really fancies you. Apparently he was being very suggestive, and saying that by the end of the—"

I put my hand up to stop her.

"Please … don't say any more. He gives me the creeps."

"I know what you mean. Tom shot him down though, told him to shut up. He told me he was going to speak to—" She stops abruptly and looks awkwardly at me.

"Speak to who?"

She looks embarrassed, and I don't want to upset her by pursuing the issue. I'm not going to upset her over James, or anyone else for that matter.

"No worries," I continue kindly. "Let's forget it, eh? Let's just get ready and go for dinner, then we'll go and enjoy the band."

She looks relieved and smiles, and I nod in response. We say no more about it, as we both make our way to our rooms to get ready.

I dress in my jeans and a grey top, nothing too fancy. I put on some heels, fasten my hair up and apply some makeup. Alison is waiting for me in the lounge. She's all dolled up, wearing a lovely pair of designer trousers and a gorgeous red jumper. She has a stunning figure hidden beneath her clothes, with curves in all the right places. She's left her hair down in long, soft curls. Her blonde tresses make her blue eyes really sparkle.

"Wow! You look beautiful."

"So do you." I shake my head at her, but she continues. "Even dressed casually you look stunning. I don't know why I'm friends with you!"

I laugh at such a ridiculous notion.

"Come on. I'm starving!"

The club isn't far, so we walk the short distance. It's quite nice inside, and larger than I'd expected. There are already quite a few people in, mainly men propping up the bar and talking about football. The band are on stage setting up – two women and three men. They have a sign over the stage that reads: *You ask, we'll play.*

"That's an odd name for a band," I say. "You ask, we'll play."

"No … they're called Variety."

I shake my head, trying not to laugh, and reply sarcastically. "Really?"

She points to the sign below their names on the poster over the bar.

"Variety, live at the Music Bar, Saturday night. You ask, we'll play," she reads.

She's not got it, that I was really taking the mickey about the band's name, so I smile and reply, "I hope they're good!"

"Me too. Tom says they are."

"What time is he coming?"

"Around ten. He's working till nine."

We sit at a table near to the dance floor. There's a menu on the table so I open it and glance over the few options available.

"There's not much choice," I comment, pulling a face.

"Let's see. Yeah, I see what you mean. Burger and chips, or cheeseburger and chips?"

"Decisions, decisions!"

"I'm sure the menu used to be better than this."

"Maybe it's because they have the band on."

"Maybe. Okay, what are you having?"

"Umm, I think I'll have the burger and chips," I say with a smile. "Have you decided yet?"

"I suppose I'll have the same." We both laugh, and I go to the bar and order our food and a glass of white wine each.

Our burgers arrive with a cheeky smile, directed at Alison, from the man behind the bar.

"Get your coat," I say with a laugh as he walks away. "You've pulled!"

She rolls her eyes at me.

"Stop it and eat your burger."

The food actually isn't that bad, but the wine would be better off on the chips.

"Another?" Alison asks as I finish my glass.

I shake my head, grimacing at the taste.

"No, thank you. I'm sure it came out of the vinegar bottle."

"Umm, it was a bit nasty, wasn't it? What about a G&T with ice?"

I think about it for just a moment.

"Why not? I don't drink much as a rule; it goes straight to my head. I'm a cheap night – burger and chips, and one glass of alcohol. How classy!"

Alison goes to the bar to order our drinks. When she returns with them, I take a sip of mine.

"Hell, that's strong! Are they doubles?"

She shakes her head, and we both look towards the stage as the band tune their instruments. The place is filling up nicely now. By the time we've had a few G&Ts, we're chatting about everything and nothing, laughing and giggling from the alcohol.

We both roll our eyes as we see Darcy and Emily arrive with James and another man. They walk past us towards the bar. James keeps looking over towards us, and it's making me feel uneasy. I get up to go to the loo.

As I come out from the ladies' toilets, along the corridor off the main room, Darcy comes through the doors and looks me up and down. I return the favour with a pointed look of my own. She's wearing a short, fitted red dress and very high heels. There's no denying how attractive she is. Her hair hangs down her back, long and straight, but her makeup is a little overdone.

"Don't you dare tell anyone what you heard today, or you'll be sorry," she snaps.

I've had several G&Ts so I'm a little more than tipsy. We're not on the ward either, which adds to my confidence.

"Really?"

Oh, she doesn't like that! The look on her face is a picture, and I wonder how infrequently anyone is defiant towards her.

She grits her teeth, nearly spitting at me.

"I'm warning you! Back off from Mr Scott and James, or I'll have you."

I feel like I'm in the playground.

"You'll what?" I sneer back at her. "I don't think so somehow …" Her face turns scarlet as I continue. "You want them? You go for it! I'm not stopping you."

She looks surprised by my response but then her expression changes, and she looks smug. I realise that she must think I've backed down. She turns on her heels, whipping her head round so her hair flies around her face, and starts to make her way back to the club. I shout to her, stopping her in her tracks.

"Darcy, I've not finished yet. I said you should go for it, but somehow I don't think your feelings will be reciprocated. Rumour has it that you're the hospital bike, desperate to bag yourself a doctor. And you've the personality of a warthog."

I smirk at her.

She throws me a dirty look and raises her hand to slap me.

I shake my head. "I wouldn't if I were you. You don't know me, or what I'm capable of with the mood I'm in. Trust me, it wouldn't be a good idea."

I don't think she can make her mind up whether to attack me or not. She puts her hand down.

"I've warned you as well. You don't know me either!"

I smirk and shrug my shoulders. I'm on a roll now, feeling both brave and pissed off at being treated like a doormat. It seems like everyone I meet thinks they can say whatever they want to me. Clones of Adam. Well, I'm not standing for it any more.

"I'm glad that we've cleared that little matter up," I say more calmly than I feel. "We don't know each other, and I certainly don't want to know you. Now you trot off back to your letch before he starts making a move on Emily."

———

151

From the look on her face, I can tell she's absolutely livid.

"You'll regret that," she snipes, almost screeching. "Bitch!"

"Yeah, yeah, whatever." I manage to keep my cool, although I'm thinking, *I'm sure I will.* I breathe deeply as she bounces out through the doors and back into the room. Hell, I've never spoken like that to anyone before, or been that confrontational. Where did that come from? I grin to myself – probably the bottle of gin. I chuckle, feeling quite proud that I've finally stuck up for myself for once in my life. No more doormat for me!

I arrive back at the table and look over to the bar. Darcy is openly groping James, holding onto him before he makes a play for anyone else.

I smile at Alison, although I'm starting to feel a little shaky. I think it's the adrenalin. I pick up my drink as I sit down, knocking it straight back and wincing at the taste.

"Are you okay? What's happened?"

I tell her, and she's laughs loudly. "Good for you! It's about time someone said something to her and put her in her place. You don't believe the rumours she's spreading around, do you, about Edward?"

I don't answer her because, honestly, I don't know what I believe any more.

Darcy can see Alison laughing, and she's not happy at all. But who cares? I certainly don't. I'm trying my best to stay positive, but Alison has just put Edward back into my head. The band starts to play another song.

"Oh, I love this song. Let's dance!"

We both get up singing along as we move with the music. The band's good, but as the song continues it starts to remind me of Edward. *"You go back to her…"*

I start thinking about the rumours that are going around the hospital. All, no doubt, started by Darcy. *He's gone to see an old girlfriend. He's smitten with her, wants to get back with her.* I shrug my shoulders ironically at myself. Would he go back to an old girlfriend? Nothing I've heard about him makes him sound like the type, and his reputation is of a one-night stand guy, so would he have even had a girlfriend? Or maybe that's why he only has one-night stands now. If he was smitten with her, maybe she broke his heart.

I sigh. God, too many questions, or am I making excuses for him now? He's probably not even got a heart. I really don't know what to think any more.

We stay on the dance floor for another three songs. Tom arrives, and Alison makes a daft noise as she sees him coming in. She waves, pointing to our table. He walks over to it and takes a seat, smiling at Alison while she makes puppy eyes at him.

"Go over and say hi," I say. "I'm fine dancing."

"Are you sure?"

"Yes, honestly."

She goes and sits with Tom, smiling away at him, and I think how nice it is that they're so much in love.

The song finishes and I clap the band. I'm really enjoying myself, despite Darcy's bitchiness and James's lechery. The bandleader announces that he has a request to play for a special lady. Out the corner of my eye I see James, Darcy, Emily and the other man coming onto the dance floor. Darcy is grinning from ear to ear, as if I'm supposed to care that she obviously thinks James has requested the song for her. She throws her arms around him as the song starts to play. I turn my back on them, pulling a face at Alison and Tom, who both laugh. I close my eyes and start to feel the music, swaying, smiling and singing to myself. It makes me think of my grandad; he loved this music. Soulful, he used to call it, although I do think my grandad had a soft spot for Diana Ross. Thanks to him, I grew up with Motown.

I'm singing away to myself when I feel a pair of arms slide around my waist from behind. I stop suddenly and open my eyes as a voice whispers into my ear. It sends a shudder down my spine.

153

"Hmm … you move well. Who's loving you, Abigail?"

I turn quickly and try to pull away from him.

"Take your hands off me, right now!" I shout.

James grins at me.

"Come on. One dance, Abigail, one dance. I know you want to." He grabs me firmly and I start to panic. He whispers into my ear, "You look so hot and sexy."

I can smell the whisky on his breath as he pulls me firmly towards him, and I immediately think of Adam. My heart is racing as I push him hard.

His voice is oily as he continues, "Don't play hard to get. I know you want to!"

He tries to kiss me, and I lose it completely.

"Take your hands off me now or I'll scream!"

He sees Alison running over, followed by Tom, and lets go of me. Alison grabs my arm and pulls me away, while Tom, who looks furious, walks over to James and says something to him. They start to argue and Darcy stalks over to me.

"I warned you, you little bitch!" she screams, raising her hand to hit me. As if any of this is my fault. She's screeching at me, calling me all sorts of names, and people have stopped dancing to watch the floorshow.

Alison takes my hand. "Come on, we're going. Tom, we're going."

He nods at her, and then says something else to James. I hear Edward's name mentioned, and Darcy looks at me with venom in her eyes, as if she wants to punch me. I don't know what's being said because Alison is moving me quickly from the dance floor and towards the table to get our bags. A moment later, Tom joins us.

"Come on, girls," Tom says kindly. "Let me walk you back to the flat."

I can still hear Darcy and James shouting at each other as we're leaving. We get outside and I start to apologise to them both.

"I'm so sorry."

"Don't you dare be sorry, Abbie! We both saw what happened, and it wasn't your fault."

I roll my eyes. What a horrible end to what was my first free night out in forever.

Tom walks us back to the flat. We enter and I go straight to the bathroom.

"I'll go home," I hear Tom say, "so that you and Abbie can talk. That was a bit out of order, what Darcy and James did."

"Okay. If you're sure that's what you want to do."

"Not really, babe, but I think Abbie needs a good friend right now."

"Yes, I suppose she does."

They both sound really disappointed. I don't want Tom to leave because of me. It's Alison's flat, and she wants him to stay. I leave the bathroom and clear my throat, speaking as firmly as I can.

"You'd better not be leaving on my account, Tom. I'm okay, I promise. I freaked out a little but, honestly, I'm fine. I'm going to go to bed, so please stay with Alison."

Alison comes over and gives me a big hug.

"Are you sure?"

I nod yes.

"Thanks, Abbie."

I say goodnight and go off to my room, quickly, before they can change their minds. I get straight into bed, although I feel like I want a shower. I keep thinking about James, what he said to me on the dance floor and in front of Darcy. They'd been dancing with each other, and he'd left her and come over to me, saying and doing what he did right in front of her. I try to get comfortable, tossing and turning, struggling to get off to sleep. I keep assaulting the pillow but it doesn't work; I just can't get comfortable – there's too much going around in my head. I close my eyes, and Edward's face appears. I open them and stare into the darkness, wondering if someone else is loving him.

I wonder where he is, and why he left the way he did. He's clearly not interested in me. Maybe they're right; maybe it is an old girlfriend. He's not been in contact, but then he doesn't have my number. He could have asked Tom to get it from Alison, but then I remember that she doesn't have my number either. He could have telephoned the ward, passed a message on, left me his number. I'm damn sure he's got that number.

Wake up and smell the coffee, I tell myself sternly. I've blown it. I can't blame him, though. I've acted like a right bitch. I don't know what's wrong with me. I'm snapping all the time, overreacting to the slightest thing. What I said about him was out of character, and I wish he hadn't overheard, but he does fluster me. He makes me feel things I've never felt before, confusing me. I just don't know any more.

I think about what I said to Darcy. I would never have said anything like that to anyone a few months ago; I'd have just walked away. I wouldn't have reacted so emotionally to Edward either. I would've hidden away, too self-conscious to show my face because of the attention he was giving me.

I realise that I am changing, and it's about time, although everything that could possibly go wrong is going wrong.

And Edward? Well, maybe he's best left well alone.

Chapter 13

I get through Sunday in a daze. I make the roast dinner and scones for Alison and Tom, although I don't eat much and only pick at my food. I'm just not hungry.

I go for a run, but that doesn't help either. I can't seem to stop thinking about Edward.

Tom asks me if I like him, but I don't answer, not knowing really what to say.

Because I do like him, but I'm also trying to forget him. The more I think about him, the more confused I am as to why he's cut all contact, leaving without a word.

Alison and I start two days of seminars tomorrow, so at least I'll not have to face James, Darcy or even Edward for that matter. I'm hoping it will give me some time to get my head together, take my mind off things. I'm only working Thursday and Friday on the wards, so I've a reprieve until then.

I have an early night, conscious of all the work I'll need to do to get through these next few days, and also knowing I have some serious decisions to make.

I close my eyes, sighing deeply. Why is nothing simple?

Alison and I walk into the seminar rooms, ready for a very long day of lectures and drillings.

"Abbie, dinner was lovely last night."

I smile but don't say anything.

"Are you all right?" Alison asks.

I nod, pondering the decision I made last night just to be friends with Edward. That's if he's even speaking to me, which I don't think he is, in which case the choice has already been made for me.

"Are you thinking about Edward?"

Hell, even my thoughts aren't private any more. Or is it just really obvious?

Darcy's kept up with the rumours about Edward and

where he's been: *seeing an old girlfriend* – those were her words. Others say that his grandad is ill, and some say his father's poorly. I've ignored them as best I can, apart from Darcy's. That one, about an old girlfriend, has stuck in my mind, although it doesn't matter where he's been or with whom, as there's no us. In fact, there never was an us, just perhaps the possibility of it. I would like to know, though, if he lied to me about liking me and wanting to know me better. My head is mush before I've even started the lectures or seminars.

Alison squeezes my hand as we take our seats.

We don't speak to each other all the way through. I just concentrate on listening to every word, making notes and underlining important information. I even join in, asking questions and answering a few. I'm trying my best to take my mind off everything.

Day one is over with, and I'm mentally drained. I have a hot bath and an early night.

Day two is the same, although Alison is quiet as well. She didn't see Tom yesterday, and isn't seeing him today, because he's on double shifts. Sister's asked if we can both do an early shift on Wednesday, as they're short-staffed. That's meant to be a study day, and, of course, I'm meant to be seeing my gran. Sister was kind and said that we can go early so that I can keep my lunch date.

Once the seminar's over, we pack our things away and head back to the flat, both of us feeling exhausted. We have some dinner together, but Alison wants an early night. We're both feeling a little miserable. Alison is pining for Tom, and I've heard nothing from Edward. I'm not even sure if he's back, though rumour has it he came back yesterday.

The following morning, I wake to the alarm clock going off. I'm shattered. I've not slept well at all, tossing and turning all night, worried about seeing Edward on the ward today, if he's back. I don't know if he'll speak to me, or even acknowledge me for that matter.

I shower, dress and wait for Alison. When she appears from her bedroom she's smiling at me, but she looks tired too.

"Are you seeing Tom tonight?" I ask.

She nods. "Yes, he rang late last night. And you, have you heard anything?"

"No, I think it's over between us." I sigh. "Not that it ever began."

She smiles and doesn't reply. Which is odd, because she normally would, and I'm now wondering if perhaps Tom told her something last night – about Edward – and she doesn't want to tell me. I don't pursue it. I don't have the energy.

We arrive on the ward and put our things away, then sit and wait for the handover. Darcy walks in, beaming and looking like the cat that got the cream. It must be Sister's day off today so that means Darcy's in charge. After the handover, she starts allocating jobs and duties. I roll my eyes, knowing that my day just got worse, if that was at all possible. Back to scrubbing the ward, bedpans, and sluice room, no doubt. I feel like bloody Cinderella.

I get the worst jobs ever, just as I expected. Collecting sputum samples and taking the warm pots to the path lab. It makes me gag and heave. Sluice duty – even some of the other nurses look surprised by that one. I'm sure she's making these jobs up as she goes along. However, I grin and bear it, cleaning the bedpans and sluice room with as much good grace as I can muster. Three bloody times! She makes a dig at me at every opportunity she gets, about me being a flirt, batting my eyelashes at anyone who takes notice, and of course about Edward and the mysterious girlfriend.

I return some results from the path lab to the nursing station, as they need recording in the patient's notes. Of course, I'm not senior enough to enter them myself, as Darcy keeps reminding me. I grit my teeth as I put them down, and she makes a sly remark to Emily, her co-conspirator.

"Mr Scott hasn't been onto the ward today. I wonder why? Oh, I know, Emily – it's probably something to do with which staff are on duty today. After all, he was here Monday and Tuesday. Don't you think he seemed really happy and talkative yesterday, telling us what he'd been up to?"

"Yes, Darcy." Emily pauses. "He's spoken to you at great length today several times on the phone."

Darcy giggles as I try to hold my temper. She's well and truly goading me. I look at the clock; it's 2 p.m. I only have to keep my cool for another half hour.

I walk off and hear her mutter, "Stupid little bitch! I'll show her."

My fists are clenched and I've bitten my lip so hard that I've drawn blood. Alison sees, and shakes her head at me.

"Don't, Abbie."

I breathe deeply to calm myself down, and walk back into bay one. I try to pass the time as quickly as possible. I look out of the window and my heart misses a beat. Edward is in the car park, presumably walking to his car. Someone stops him, a man, and he talks to him. He laughs, making me want to knock on the window and shout out to him. He looks happy and carefree. I close my eyes, thinking about what might have been. When I open them again, he's gone. I feel sad, nervous and jittery, and my heart is racing.

Alison calls to me, "Come on, we can go!"

I go to the staff room and get my bag. I've survived another day, but my heart is aching.

We head back to the flat. I shower quickly and change, and we both go to meet my gran in town. We sit at her usual table in the deli. I smile at her as she talks the socks off Alison, thanking her for helping me, although she's mentioned several times that I could have gone to her instead. I roll my eyes at her each time she says it, and she shakes her head back at me. Alison and Gran get on like a house on fire, which I knew they would. I'm pretty quiet myself, although I join in the conversation occasionally – when I can get a word in edgeways.

"You're quiet today, Abbie. Are you okay, love?"

Alison is about to say something, but I glare at her, and she smiles and blushes. I think she's just realised that I probably don't want her to mention Edward.

"Oh, Mrs Baxter, we've had the most terrible two days of grilling in the seminars. It was enough to make even the chattiest of people quiet."

I grin at her. *Okay, you got yourself out of that one.*

"Oh, call me Elizabeth, please." Gran must like her.

We've finished our food and our second lattes. It's dark outside and pouring with rain.

Gran looks at her watch. "My goodness, is that the time? I'll have to dash. William is picking me up. It's bridge night tonight instead of Thursday, because Mrs McGuire has a hospital appointment tomorrow. She's thrown everybody's routine out of the window."

"Oh, Gran," I say, laughing.

"What's so funny?" she demands.

"Nothing. It's just that, well, that was a lot of information."

"You know me, Abbie. If I can say ten words instead of three, I will."

I just grin and get up to help her on with her mac.

"You're a good girl," she says fondly, and I smile.

"I've had a good teacher."

She squeezes my hand and I realise that her grip is not as strong as it used to be. I pull the collar up on her mac, moving her hair from underneath it, and smile at her.

"Hey now. What's all this? Are you okay?"

I nod, but I realise that I'm looking down on her now, not up as I once did. As I look into her eyes, I see that they don't sparkle as they used to do. They used to shine like pools of blue in the sun. They'd captivate you as she talked. She could tell stories with those eyes.

She takes my hand, smiling, and it feels small in mine. I

can feel the wrinkles and veins. Tears fill my eyes as it hits me that she's getting old. Her hair was once chestnut brown and shimmered like silk.

Grandad loved her hair, and would say: "You should wear a warning sign when you go out, Elizabeth. That hair of yours could cause an accident, it shines so bright. It's dazzling in the sun. And you know something else? You could give any of those fifties pinups a run for their money! You're just beauty itself."

She'd reply, "Don't be silly, George. Get out of here."

He'd laugh, and she'd beam from ear to ear, winking at me. I'd giggle, not really knowing what they were talking about, but I know now what his words meant to her, and what her giggles meant to him. They meant love. Grandad would have been eighty this year. I miss him so much – his sayings, his kind ways, his humour, his love, and especially his hugs. Grandad's hugs always made everything better.

It's true, though, what he said about Gran. She is beautiful, and the nicest thing about my gran is that her beauty isn't just skin-deep. I hug her to me tightly. She'll be seventy on New Year's Day. Why am I feeling like this?

"Abbie, what is wrong? What aren't you telling me?"

"Nothing, Gran. I just miss you so much, that's all."

She looks at me and shakes her head. She's not stupid, and she knows me too well.

"I'm fine, honest."

"And so am I."

She kisses me on the cheek as the door to the deli opens.

"William's here now. I'll see you to the car, Gran."

The staff, all twelve of them, call out, "Night, Mrs Baxter. Bye, Abigail."

Alison looks puzzled, but she smiles at me anyway. I grab an umbrella and walk outside with Gran. I hold her tight to me, with the brolly over her, sheltering her from the rain as it pelts at me. William opens the door and she bends forward to get into the passenger side. I move forward and help her in.

"I'm not falling apart, I'll have you know."

"I know, but will you ring me, please, when you get home? Then I know you've got back safely."

"Oh, dear me, Abbie. What's come over you?" She smiles, and then continues, "But, yes, I will."

"I'll make sure she gets in safe, Abigail."

"Thank you, William."

"Hell's bells and buckets of blood, you two!" She's not said that for a long time, and I know she's a little annoyed with us both. She's very independent and fit for her age, she still goes into work every day, Monday through to Friday, and insists on making the final decisions on the board. "I'm not about to push up the daisies yet!"

I laugh, rolling my eyes.

"I know you're not. Now come on. Don't be stubborn." I smile at her affectionately, and she shakes her head with a chuckle.

"Stubborn! If I wasn't in such a rush, young lady — "

"Well, you are in a rush, remember?" I interrupt. "So please ring me when you get in. And Gran …" I pause, smiling at her. "I love you."

She shakes her head at me.

"I love you too. Goodnight and God bless."

"Goodnight and God bless, Gran."

William gets into the car, and Gran waves at me as the Bentley drives off down the high street.

My brolly has blown inside out, and the spokes are sticking out through the material. It's a goner. As I walk a little way up the street to the bin, a couple attracts my attention. They're laughing and running, holding hands in the rain. They stop and kiss each other, then continue running. She suddenly screams as he drags her into a shop doorway, holding her tight, sheltering her from the rain and kissing her. I suddenly feel like I'm prying. I look away and wonder if this is what my life will be like. Is it my fate to watch other people being happy, without ever having that happiness myself?

Alison makes me jump.

"Come on, Abbie. What are you doing? You're soaking wet."

"Sorry, I'm coming."

We get in Alison's car. She's looking at me, puzzled.

"Abbie, I went to pay the bill, but the staff just looked at me funny and said it was on the house."

I glance at her and say nothing.

"Abbie?"

"They would say that."

"Why? Did you already pay?"

"Something like that."

Her eyes go wide and she frowns as she cottons on.

"Oh my God, Abbie, I've just realised – Baxter's deli ..."

I smile wearily as she continues, "The whole chain?"

I close my eyes. What do I say?

"Keep it quiet, please. I don't like people knowing, they ... well, they treat you differently." I sigh. "Very differently. Their intentions towards you ... aren't always good, especially when they find out about the money. As I've learnt."

"Adam?"

I nod, and she pats my leg.

"I understand. I'll not say anything, I promise." She pauses, raising her eyebrows. "You're certainly a dark horse."

We don't say another word about it as we drive back to the flat. We toss a coin to see who gets the shower first, and Alison wins. I take off my wet clothes and put on my dressing gown. Then I make us both a hot milky drink while I wait for Alison to finish in the bathroom.

"It's all yours, Abbie. I'll probably be gone when you come out. I'm not stopping at Tom's tonight, and I'll not be late home."

"Okay," I shout back as I run my bath. "I'll most likely watch a bit of telly and have an early night myself. See you in the morning."

"Okay, and if your gran rings you, please tell her I had a

lovely lunch, and it was so nice to meet her. She's lovely!"

"Thanks, I will. Have a nice time. I know you've been looking forward to seeing Tom."

I smile to myself, pleased that Alison likes Gran. She is lovely, I think.

When I've had my hot bath, I sit and watch a drama on the telly. It's a murder mystery about a serial killer. I turn if off halfway through, as it keeps making me jump.

Gran telephones me to say she got home safely. I pass on the message from Alison, and she returns the compliment. We chat for a short while but she has to say goodbye earlier than normal, as her friends from the bridge club are arriving.

I go to my room for yet another early night. I'm tired tonight, not physically but mentally. I smile at the knitted rabbit on my pillow, and pick it up and hug it to me as I climb into bed. My head hits the pillow and tears suddenly sting my eyes. I love my gran so much. I would be lost without her. I need to stop thinking such dark thoughts. I curl myself up into a ball, holding the knitted rabbit to my chest, feeling sad and lonely. Extremely lonely, and with such a heavy heart.

I close my eyes. Why do I feel like I'm losing everyone?

Chapter 14

I wake in the morning feeling very strange. My hands are shaking and I feel cold. My tummy is churning, as if I'm going to be sick. I feel nervous and anxious. I sit at the table in the lounge, waiting for Alison and fidgeting with the strap on my bag. My legs are dancing under the table, and I can't keep them still. Alison comes into the lounge.

"Are you ready, Abbie?"

I jump.

"Sorry, are you okay? You look shattered."

I smile and reply, lying through my back teeth, "Yes, I'm fine."

She gives me an odd look, but I keep smiling at her.

"Come on, then."

Alison and I sit in the handover, taking notes from the night sister. She's explaining how the patients have been overnight.

"Mrs Baker may be discharged today, although Mr Scott wants to see her first before he makes his final decision."

Darcy makes a comment under her breath about Mr Scott being on the ward today, and something about me.

"Nice one. He's back with his old girlfriend now and seems really content and happy. There'll probably be wedding bells soon, so I'm told."

I try my best to ignore her and keep my head down. When the handover is finished, we all start to get up, but Sister asks us to wait as the night team leave.

"Firstly, we are short-staffed in clinic today, so I need one of the students to go and help out. Alison, will you go please?"

"Yes, that's fine, Sister."

Darcy frowns.

"Sister, would Abigail not be better off going to the clinic? Alison has far more experience here on the ward."

Sister glances at Darcy but doesn't respond to her comment.

"Thank you, Alison."

Darcy doesn't challenge her.

Sister continues, "We're admitting a patient today, a Mrs Abbott, who has throat cancer. She's one of Mr Scott's patients, although her treatment today on the ward is not for her throat cancer, it's for her bilateral leg ulcers. Mr Scott has spoken to Mr Andrew, and he's agreed for her to stay here on our ward instead of going to the Day Case Unit. I know this isn't normal procedure, but Mr Scott wants her here so that we can monitor her. She's a close friend of his, so a little word of warning: be pleasant, kind and mindful of your nursing skills with her, as she's a retired doctor. She's extremely anxious and worried about the procedure. Darcy, can you admit Mrs Abbott? I have to be in theatre this morning. You can take Abigail with you; it's a good learning opportunity for her."

I don't know whether to be flattered or flummoxed, but then think, *Super. A full day with the warthog.* Darcy doesn't look pleased about it either. I see Emily nudge her, and Darcy's lips pull into a grimace. Sister waits for a response from Darcy as the door opens.

Edward walks into the room. He looks at Sister and nods, then glances quickly at me, before looking away equally quickly. I feel my body tense as I put my head down.

He addresses Sister, his voice tetchy. "Sister, what time is the courier arriving?"

"Around eleven o'clock, Mr Scott."

He just nods curtly.

"I know you're helping out in theatre today, so who'll be admitting Mrs Abbott?"

Sister doesn't get a chance to reply.

"I am, Mr Scott."

He nods at Darcy, and she smiles back flirtatiously at him.

167

"Can you page me when the package arrives?"

"Yes, of course, Mr Scott." She's beaming from ear to ear. He doesn't look at me and I'm slowly getting the message. "Is Mrs Abbott here on the ward, Mr Scott?"

"Yes, she's in my office."

He leaves the room. I might as well have been invisible.

We all leave the handover, and Alison taps my arm.

"Are you going to be okay?"

"I've no choice, have I? I wish I was in clinic instead of you. That was more than awkward."

"I'd better go. Chin up. I'm sorry it's not working out with … See you after your shift."

I'm sure now that Edward has spoken to Tom about me. He's not interested any more, and it's obvious that Alison didn't want to tell me last night. I smile at her as she leaves, and then I get an earful from Darcy.

"Oh dear, Abbie. Are you not flavour of the month any more? What does that feel like?" she says mockingly.

I want to scream at her, but I can't. It's my job and she's my mentor. If I give her an inch then she'd take a mile, and I know she'd use it against me.

She shouts orders at me – a mammoth job list: clean the bedpans, make the beds, clean the beds, run to the pharmacy, run to the path lab, go back to the pharmacy, go back to the path lab, clean more bedpans. My head is spinning.

There's no time for a break, although she goes for one herself.

They're returning from their break, walking up the corridor, when Emily spots me and nudges Darcy.

"Come on, hurry up! Why are you dawdling around?" Darcy snaps as I'm entering the sluice room with a full bedpan. I'm tempted, very tempted, to tip it over her head.

I come back out of the sluice needing a wee, and head into the staff toilets. I'm in one of the cubicles when I hear Darcy and Emily come in and put their bags away. Emily is speaking to Darcy.

"Well, what have you done this time, Darcy? Have you fixed it?" she says, sniggering.

"Have I! I did that Saturday night. The silly cow doesn't know what she's let herself in for. She won't cross me again in a hurry."

I try to think. Saturday night, she did what?

She continues cheerfully. "It's all working out just fine and dandy, and she can chaperone Mrs Abbott today. I'm sure she'll leave after that."

They both laugh as they leave. I wait a few moments, trying to calm myself down, then leave.

"Go round to room two," Darcy shouts at me as I come out of the toilets.

I close my eyes. I'm not sure how much longer I can hold my temper.

I enter room two and find Mrs Abbott sitting in her chair. She's about sixty, very well dressed, with grey hair tied back from her face. Nice features. I bet she was stunning in her day. Both of her legs, from her feet to as far as I can see, have been bandaged. She smiles.

"Hi," I say warmly, trying to put her at ease. "I'm Abigail, a student nurse."

She looks nervous, and I feel sorry for her straight away.

"Are you worried about the procedure?"

She nods her head, patting her hand on the bed for me to sit.

"Yes, dear, I am." She's polite and extremely well spoken. She takes a deep breath as she continues. "I've never liked maggots."

My eyes are like saucers.

"Haven't they told you what I'm having done?"

I shake my head. Bloody hell, maggots! Oh God, I can't stay for this. She takes my hand.

"Well, these ulcers" – she points towards her legs – "won't heal because of the cancer. So this is my only option now, or they'll have to amputate my legs."

"Oh dear, that's awful," I say sympathetically.

She gives me a warm smile.

"It's a good learning project for you, and very interesting. I'm sure you'll not see this sort of thing again."

I don't want to see it at all! I look at the clock and see that it's 11.15 a.m. That's what the courier must be delivering. Oh, Darcy is a right bitch! My hands have started to sweat.

I whisper, "May I just wash my hands, Mrs Abbott?"

I need a few minutes to psych myself up for this.

"Of course you may."

"Thank you."

I go into the bathroom and close the door. I lean against it. Holy shit! I don't want to stay and see this. I need to hide, but there's nowhere to go apart from the bin. I look at it for a moment. I even contemplate getting in, but I won't fit. Bugger, bugger, bugger! I'm having a panic attack. Breathe, Abbie, breathe. I hear Darcy coming into the room, turning on the charm.

"Hello, Mrs Abbott. Can I please ask you some questions and take your observations?"

"Of course, my dear."

I hear the BP machine going as Darcy talks to Mrs Abbott.

"All fine there, Mrs Abbott."

I'm still hiding in the bathroom, being very, very, quiet and hoping no will notice or hear me.

Darcy continues. "Your pulse is a little elevated."

Mrs Abbott breathes deeply, sounding nervous when she speaks.

"Umm, yes, I'm not fond of maggots, as I was just telling your colleague. She's in there, washing her hands."

No, don't tell her that, for God's sake! I hear Edward's voice in the room.

"Oh, Mr Scott, I didn't realise you were coming back."

That's all I need.

He asks Darcy if all the observations are okay.

"Yes, Mr Scott, all fine apart from her pulse. That was a

little elevated at ninety-two." She breathes a deep sigh of satisfaction, but his voice is flat when he replies.

"Okay, you can leave now, Darcy."

"Oh, okay." She sounds disappointed.

"Oh Edward!" Mrs Abbott exclaims. "Come here and give me a hug. I have missed you!"

I hear another knock at the door, and another voice.

"Hello, Mrs Abbott. I'm Gail from the tissue-viability team. Am I okay to take you through to the treatment room?"

Mrs Abbott's voice sounds panicky as she replies, "They've arrived then?"

I take a deep breath.

"Yes, Mrs Abbott, they've arrived, and on time too!"

I hear Edward speaking gently.

"Here, let me help you, Edwina."

"You're such a sweet boy, Edward!"

I roll my eyes. The bathroom door opens unexpectedly and I suddenly find myself falling backwards into the room. I'm flapping my arms around like a windmill, trying to steady myself. Someone grabs my arm and steadies me. I look round to see who it is and find myself face to face with a stunning woman in her late twenties. She's holding my arm and looking at me with surprise. I grin apologetically at her. She's beautiful, with long dark hair, big blue eyes, and she's dressed immaculately in what looks like a designer suit, navy blue with a pale-pink blouse. She's even wearing killer heels. She looks like a model and has a fantastic figure. When she speaks, her voice is soft.

"Oh, I'm so sorry! Are you okay? I didn't know anyone was in there."

I smile timidly at her. Everyone is looking at me, and I really want to leave. My face burns red again. Edward is staring at me, shaking his head in disapproval, but Mrs Abbott is kind. She can see I'm in a tizzy, and seems quite amused by it.

"There you are, my dear. I thought you'd got lost."

171

I smile at her, wishing I had done.

"You can help me now, please, Abigail." She holds out her hand to me. "You'll have a good view of what they're doing."

Oh great!

I walk over to her, still smiling. I have to walk past Edward, who moves out of my way, but still doesn't speak to me. I'm slowly but surely getting the message.

"Edward, are you coming to watch?"

"Not really my cup of tea, Edwina. I'll take Fiona for a coffee and pop back to see you later." He moves his arm around Fiona's waist, guiding her out of the room. Fiona smiles back at Edward.

"I'll see you soon, Mother."

I study the two of them as I help Mrs Abbott out of her chair. Mother; close friend. Close friend to whom, Mrs Abbott or her daughter, Fiona? Could this be the mysterious girlfriend? They smile at each other as they leave the room, and I'm suddenly feeling jealous as hell! Why can't I stop thinking like this? I want that smile to be for me. I shouldn't; I've no logical reason to feel jealous. He never promised me anything, apart from the things he said to me in my room, and then at the flat. But I'm jealous all the same.

I'll wait until you're ready. I don't want to leave.

He's a player all right, and playing me like a bloody fiddle.

My face has flushed again, but this time in frustration. He looks at me, and I wonder if he's trying to provoke me, because it's bloody working. Who was I kidding? He does affect me, he affects me badly, or why would I be feeling like this? My throat has gone very dry. I swallow hard, trying to release some saliva before my eyes start watering. My hand starts to shake, and I put it behind my back quickly before anyone sees. Then I watch them walking off down the corridor, his hand in the small of her back. I want to kick myself for being pulled into his web. I'm so glad I asked him to leave. He seems very close to Fiona, and she looks more his type than I do.

I enter the treatment room with Mrs Abbott and the tissue-viability nurse. Mrs Abbott takes a seat, and Gail starts to remove the dressings on her legs. The smell is unbearable, like rotting flesh, which I suppose is exactly what it is. I gag, and hope she hasn't seen me do this. Darcy comes in with a box, handing it to Gail.

"Aww, didn't Mr Scott look happy!"

She smiles smugly at me, and I know what she's referring to. That comment was aimed squarely at me, not Gail.

"Are you not staying, Darcy?" Gail asks.

"Oh no, I'm far too busy, Gail," she replies in a voice full of her own self-importance. "I've a ward to run for Mr Scott!"

She leaves the room.

Gail smiles at Mrs Abbott. "Are you ready?"

She nods her head, squeezing my hand so tightly that I feel the blood draining from it.

Gail removes the maggots from the box and places them on a sterile field. They're wriggling around in a net. She starts prodding them with tweezers, counting them; one, two, three, and so on. She does the same with the other net. She's talking to herself and flicking through the paperwork that came with the box.

"Twenty in each, that's correct. We don't want to lose any."

I'm nearly crying now at the thought of it. I shiver, and she grins at me. She has a dreadful sense of humour, I think sourly.

Gail places the net carefully on the wound and starts prodding the maggots a little with the tweezers, until she's happy they're in the right place.

"That's good, they're all attached."

I'd hate her job.

Every now and again, Gail murmurs a question.

"Are you okay there, Mrs Abbott?"

Mrs Abbott doesn't answer, but keeps her eyes closed and

continues to squeeze the life out of my hand.

I want to be sick. I close my eyes as Gail repeats the same procedure on the other leg.

"What's happening, Abigail?" Mrs Abbott asks.

Oh, please don't make me look again, please!

I take a very deep breath. I open my eyes, although my brain is screaming at me to keep them closed, and it's not a pretty sight. I have to look, though, because I feel so sorry for her.

The sight that greets me makes me heave. My eyes start watering, and I can't make them stop. I feel so bad, but I can't help it. I'm not cut out to do this job. No wonder no one else came in! That cow, Darcy, knew exactly what she was doing. The maggots are bearing down, wriggling around with their behinds in the air. They remind me of piranhas feasting on their prey. It's a frenzy, a free for all. They're devouring the rotting flesh; pus and blood from the ulcer ooze down her legs. And the smell – it's like nothing I've ever encountered. It hits the back of my throat and burns; I can almost taste it. My eyes are sting and I think I'm going to be sick.

I gag again and put my hand to my mouth.

"I'm sorry!" I cry out.

I run from the room, still with my hand over my mouth to hold back the vomit. I can hear laughing as I run into the toilet and throw up. Water streams from my eyes, and I can't stop retching, or shake those images from my head. I try to compose myself, feeling bad that I've run out on Mrs Abbott. I need to go and apologise to her. I take some deep breaths and sit for about fifteen minutes until my stomach has settled.

I only had to watch; Mrs Abbott has to have them bandaged to her legs for three days.

I leave the toilet and head towards the treatment room. It's empty. I go to Mrs Abbott's room and knock on the door.

"Come in," she shouts.

Gail is just leaving as I enter. She smiles, although I don't know why. I thought she'd be mad because I ran out.

"I'm sorry," I mouth, but she grins back at me.

"I was just saying to Mrs Abbott that you lasted a lot longer than most. If you ever want a job with me, I'd be more than happy to give you one." She winks, showing me that wicked sense of humour again.

"Thanks, but no thanks," I say with a laugh.

"Well, if you change your mind, you know where to find me," she remarks with laughter in her voice, before leaving.

I walk into the room still smiling, but stop when I see Edward sitting on the bed next to Fiona. He's talking to Mrs Abbott, and they all look very cosy together. She smiles as she sees me.

"Abigail!"

Edward turns to look at me.

"What a star you are. Thank you, my dear, for your help."

I smile at her, trying not to look at Edward. I can feel myself blushing, and the tension is unbearable. I want to back out of the room.

"What can I do for you?" she enquires.

"I just wanted to say sorry, and to see if you were okay."

"I am, dear. And I can't feel a thing. And there's no need to be sorry – you were marvellous! No one else would come in. You should be proud of yourself. Shouldn't she, Edward?"

I still can't bring myself to look at him, so I nod back to Mrs Abbott and head for the door. I hear him get up behind me as I'm leaving. He follows me into the corridor, and grabs my wrist. His voice is quiet but firm.

"Hey!"

I turn, pulling my arm away and shaking my head. I frown, not answering. Then I turn my back to him and start walking down the corridor, leaving him standing there. So now he wants to talk to me? On his terms? I don't think so. He can't ignore me for nearly a week, then expect to talk, just like that.

Sister's back on the ward and has seen what's just happened.

"Abigail, go on down to the clinic and find Alison, please. You can both go and have your lunch."

I do as she says, and we make our way to the canteen. Alison quizzes me all the way there about the maggot therapy. In the end, I have to tell her to stop. She roars with laughter, but I don't see the funny side. On top of that, my mind is now full of thoughts about Edward. Did I do the right thing, pulling away like that?

We arrive at the canteen, grab a tray and join the queue. I get a cup, place it under the machine, and press for iced water. I put it on my tray with my purse and continue moving slowly in the queue.

"I fancy something hot today," Alison says from her place in front of me. "What about you?"

We reach the hot-food section, and the canteen lady starts to remove the lids. The first dish is a curry, but when she removes the second lid I have to close my eyes tight shut. It's rice. I start to get flashbacks, and when I open my eyes again the rice looks like it's moving. I start to gag, thinking of the maggots. I watch her as she puts the spoon into the rice and places it on the plate. I think I'm going to throw up again. I turn fast, needing to leave the queue, but as I do, I knock my tray into someone standing close behind me. My cup goes flying off my tray and the water spills over his trousers. My purse follows, bouncing onto the floor, bursting open and spilling my money everywhere.

I get on my hands and knees and begin to pick up the coins. Edward bends down to help me.

He moves his mouth to my ear and whispers, "It seems you don't want to talk to me, Abigail."

I blush furiously, and my hands start to shake as he moves closer to me and murmurs seductively into my ear again, "Hmm! But it seems you're destined to get my trousers off."

He stands back up, and I look up at him from the floor, still on my hands and knees.

An involuntary whimper leaves my mouth. God, he affects me so damn much! He looks amused.

"I'm sorry," I mouth, as I see his wet trousers.

He nods at me, holding out his hand. I take it and he helps me to my feet, pulling me closer.

"I need to talk to you," he says quietly.

I'm a little taken aback.

"Why now? When you've ignored me all this time?"

He stares and asks again, "Please, Abigail, let me talk to you."

"I'm not sure we have anything to say to each other."

His eyes raise, as he asks again.

"Please!"

He takes my hand and squeezes it gently. I close my eyes briefly, knowing that I'm going to go with him as he starts moving me from the queue towards the exit. I look back at Alison, who just shrugs her shoulders.

"You can't do this to me, Edward. It's not fair. You ignore me, and then choose to speak to me only when it suits you."

He stays silent, wary of the people milling around us. He walks outside with me, still holding my hand, and then stops a little way down the path where there's a little more privacy.

"When have I ignored you?" He looks confused. Is he serious? He knows he's ignored me.

"You know you have. You haven't contacted me, or said where you were – nothing. You just left without so much as a by your leave."

He looks baffled.

I continue, "Why the confused expression, Edward, when it's true?"

"Didn't you get the message I left for you on the ward on Thursday night?"

I stare at him, saying nothing.

He raises an eyebrow at me. "You texted me on Saturday night."

I shake my head, confused.

"I didn't get a message from you, and I certainly haven't texted you. How could I when I haven't got your number?"

He frowns at me, as if he's trying to work something out. He closes his eyes for a second, then opens them and shakes his head.

"Can I see you tonight?" he asks quickly. "I need to explain things to you. I've just realised what's going on, but I need to confirm something first."

I don't know what to do.

"I'm not sure it's a good idea." I'm thinking about Fiona and her mother sitting in the hospital room. He grins at me, guessing my thoughts.

"Abigail, Fiona is my sister-in-law. She's married to my brother, Simon, and Mrs Abbott, her mother, is one of my old lecturers from university. I trained to be a doctor at Bart's, where she taught. So, look, please let me see you tonight, and I'll explain everything."

I'm really mixed up now. I don't know what's going on.

"Who did you leave the message with? The one you left for me on Thursday?"

"I need to go, but can I explain tonight?" His eyes implore me to say yes as he edges away from me.

He's like a magnet. I'm drawn to him, unable to resist.

He walks back towards me, staring straight into my eyes. "Tonight?"

My heart races; I can almost feel it in my throat. I've never felt like this before. He keeps on staring at me, and his eyes are hooded and mysterious. I can't read them, can't see into them. I don't know what he's seeing or thinking, but I'm almost certain he can read my thoughts. I try to look away, feeling mixed up and confused, but my gaze is locked on his. He entrances me, drawing me in to his space, his world, and I want to go. I want to experience these feelings again and again. I'm being pulled like a moth to a flame, and I'm frightened I'll burn. I've butterflies dancing the fandango in my tummy. I try to move back, but he shakes his head at me.

"Are you going to answer me, Abigail? My trousers are wet, and I need to change."

A silly gurgle leaves my throat as he continues, "Well, can I see you later?" He tilts his head to one side, smiling at me as he waits for my response.

I think I'm going to shake my head, but, no, to my surprise I nod instead.

He nods back at me. "Good, I'll pick you up at Alison's flat."

He leaves me standing there, flummoxed, as I watch him walking back to the ward.

I go back inside to find Alison. I'm a little dazed by what's just happened. I stare out of the window as Alison eats her curry and rice, chatting away to me.

"Are you going to meet him later?"

I don't respond, I'm not sure whether I'm doing the right thing. I'm in a real dilemma. My brain says one thing, but my heart says another. I'm in a canoe up the Suwannee River with no bloody paddle! I'm pretty sure he's going to hurt me, but can I be certain of that? Can we be certain of anything in our lives, or is it all just down to fate? Does fate decide our future? Is it already mapped out for us, set in stone, or do we get to decide? I don't know any more, but one thing I do know is how he makes me feel. I know that he *does* make me feel. I feel alive for the first time in my life, and that can only be a good thing, right?

I smile to myself. *Okay, Abbie, leave it to fate.*

Alison watches me, waiting for my reply. I flash her a nervous grin.

"Well, it's looking that way! I can't seem to say no to him."

She raises her eyebrow at me, and I know she's thinking the same thing I am. That I'm putty in his hands.

Chapter 15

I walk back to the ward with Alison, reflecting on what's just happened with Edward and wondering if I've made the right decision about meeting him later. I keep asking myself the same question. Is he good for me? One minute I think it's a great idea because he makes my pulse race, excites me, and awakens the inner darkness and passion in me. The next, the whole business scares the living daylights out of me.

He says he telephoned the ward and left me a message, but I didn't receive any message. And I'm supposed to have left him a text message on Saturday night. It makes no sense, but he says he'll explain it all to me later.

I'm going to see him tonight! My pulse accelerates, blood races to my face, and my core constricts tighter than a hangman's noose at the thought. I'm in such a flap. It's true, I can't say no to him. I want to, but I can't. When he touches me, or speaks to me, he captivates me. Alison glances at me.

"Penny for them?"

I just smile as we enter the ward.

Without warning, Darcy marches towards me, mouthing, "You bitch!" She grabs my arm and starts pulling me into an empty side room. I'm so startled that I drop my bag. She slams the door shut with her foot, then flies at me in a rage, her face almost touching mine. I've no idea why she's screaming at me but before I can ask she slaps me hard across my face.

I wince, too shocked to speak. She's caught the wound on my head and it's stinging like crazy. She's absolutely enraged, nearly foaming at the mouth as she continues to scream "bitch" at me. I'm so appalled by her behaviour that I've yet to react.

"What do you think you're doing, going on a date with Mr Scott?" she shrieks in my face. "I warned you!"

"What?" I shout.

She's hit me because he said he'd see me later?

"You heard me, you cow!"

I can hear people outside in the corridor. Alison's trying to open the door, shouting my name.

I don't think about what I'm doing. Who does she think she is? I'm so mad that I pull my hand back and smack her back across her face, hard. I've never physically hit anyone before, though I've wanted to. But she's asked for it – she's crazy!

She screams again, and lunges at me. The door suddenly flies open to the room and I fall backwards into the corridor and onto the floor.

She bends and whispers into my ear, "I'll have you, you little bitch."

I stare at her in disbelief. Dear Lord, she's deranged, has totally lost the plot. Everyone has stopped to watch, and now Sister is marching down the ward with a face like thunder.

Darcy's expression changes as she sees Sister. She starts shaking her head towards her, wiping at her eyes and holding one hand to the side of her face. It looks like I've attacked her.

People have started talking. One asks, "What's happened?"

"I'm sure a student has just attacked Darcy," they reply, shocked.

I'm shaking my head. *Oh God, that's so untrue.*

"You two, in my office right now!" Sister says, firmly but discreetly.

Darcy follows Sister and Alison helps me off the floor. I roll my eyes at her in amazement. Darcy's so sly and clever. Nobody heard her, or saw what she did to me first inside the room. The whole situation seems ridiculous, but was evidently planned meticulously by her to get me into trouble.

I walk towards the office in a daze, thinking that Sister probably isn't going to believe me. It's Darcy's word against mine, and she's the deputy sister. I knock hesitantly on the door and enter.

Darcy throws me the dirtiest look ever and then, with an Oscar-winning performance, she bursts into tears.

"Sister, she hit me first," she sobs dramatically. "I was just defending myself. She's a thing for Mr Scott, and when she saw me, she went mad and started screaming at me, dragging me into the side room so that nobody could see what she was saying or doing to me."

My jaw drops, and I'm astounded by how plausible she sounds. I think she knows her job might be on the line given how she's just behaved. Sister won't fall for that, surely.

"Abigail, have you anything to say?"

Like what? You're not going to believe me over her.

I shake my head in a daze.

"Right, Abigail, you can leave. Get your bag and finish early."

I feel like screaming now, but I don't. I just shrug my shoulders and roll my eyes.

Sister sees this and says, "Go home. I'll see you on the early shift tomorrow." Her voice sounds normal, not angry as I'd expect.

As I'm leaving I catch a little of her conversation with Darcy. "One more stunt like that from you, Darcy, and—"

I don't hear the rest.

I walk past Mrs Baker's room and see that it's empty. She's been discharged. I feel a flash of disappointment; I promised I'd meet her children and say goodbye to her. I walk off the ward with my bag over my shoulder. My head's smarting, my arse is hurting, and I'm furious with Darcy for making me break my promise to Mrs Baker. I'm muttering every swearword that I know, oblivious to the fact that people are staring at me. I'm bloody seething though, to the point where I've developed tunnel vision.

I arrive at the flat and see a huge bouquet of flowers sitting on the step. I pick them up and glance at the card.

"Abigail, I'm sorry!"

"Adam, you're sick," I mutter to myself as I throw them next to the bins and walk into the building.

I enter the flat and go straight to my bedroom. I rip off my uniform, put on my running things and head straight back out of the door in a matter of seconds.

I'm running so bloody fast that I nearly fall over twice, and before I know it I've reached the park. I'm surprised to realise that I've run a mile in just a few minutes. Eat your heart out, Sir Roger Bannister, though I'm pretty sure if he'd trained as a medical student here, and not in London, he'd have done it in three minutes, not four.

I start to smile for some strange reason, thinking: I want a new job. I'm not cut out for this. I can't cope with the sick, blood and smells. A shiver runs over me as I remember the maggots. I can't even seem to stay on my own two feet either. I've completely alienated the entire hospital. No one speaks to me, and I've attracted the most handsome, but perilous man I've ever met. Oh, Abbie you can pick 'em, girl! Come to think about it, though, he picked me. Why? This still puzzles me, because he could have any woman he wanted, and I'm sure they'd do anything he asked of them and be far more willing than me. I'm doing it again; I can't seem to stop thinking about him. I shake my head, trying to dismiss my thoughts of him. I start running back to the flat.

A black BMW pips its horn at me on the main road, and pulls over. The window goes down on the passenger side, and Edward grins at me. He's like Mr Ben; I think of him, and then he appears. Hmm! That could come in useful.

"Can I pick you up at seven, Abigail?"

He's very cocky as I smile back at him. He has such a beautiful smile, and he's so seductive that I'm well aware I'm blushing. I want to say something witty to him, but I can't think of anything.

"Seven it is, then!" he replies, as I've not answered him. He raises an eyebrow at me, waiting for me to respond, but when I don't he just nods his head, a smirk on his face. "Off you trot, then. I want to watch you run in those tight pants," he says, almost growling.

It makes me blush again, and I know he's bad, and loves

making me feel uncomfortable and embarrassed. I shake my head, rolling my eyes as I turn away from him with the biggest grin on my face.

I start to run, but his car hasn't moved. It slowly sets off, and I can hear it coming up behind me. The window is still down on the passenger side as he pulls alongside me. I throw my head up into the air, trying my best not to laugh.

"You can get arrested for kerb-crawling!" I turn to him, and the look in his eyes is so hot it makes me tingle.

He speaks, his voice low and sexy. It sends shivers down my spine.

"Oh, Abigail, I could get arrested right now for what I'm thinking!" He shakes his head at me, revs the engine and shouts, "Fantastic arse, Abigail! Seven o'clock, and don't keep me waiting."

Then he drives off. Wow! He makes my head spin. I'm not sure whether I've any run left in me now.

I arrive back at the flat, and Alison pounces on me as I open the door.

"Bloody hell!" I gasp. "You scared me half to death."

"Sorry, Abbie, I didn't mean to. I was just a bit worried about you. Something happened on the ward when we were at lunch – I don't know what – but I think it was something to do with Mr Scott, Emily and Darcy. When you left, Mr Scott called Sister into his office, and there were a lot of raised voices, though I couldn't really make out what was being said. Sister sent Darcy home after that."

I shake my head.

"I've no idea what's going on either, but I'm sure I'll find out tonight. What a bloody mess."

I sigh, and start to giggle.

"What are you laughing at, Abbie?"

"I've no idea any more, but it's nice to laugh, good for the soul – isn't that what they say? It keeps the heart strong, and the way things keep happening around here, you need a strong heart."

She looks at me, surprised.

I stick my tongue out at her, and she begins to laugh herself. Once we've started we can't stop. My belly aches as we slump on the sofa together, breathless.

"I'm seeing Edward tonight," I say casually.

"Really, you're going?" I nod my head at her. "Good for you! What time?"

"He's picking me up at seven."

"Oh, really!" She raises her eyebrows. "That'll give Darcy something to think about."

"Huh, don't you mean Norman Bates?"

She holds her hand up, bringing it down with a clenched fist, repeating the movement and making a slashing noise.

"Bloody hell, don't put that thought in my head. My imagination's vivid enough without any encouragement."

She pulls a cringe-face at me and then smiles.

"I'm going for a shower," I huff.

She does it again.

"Ha ha, very funny, Alison." I grin. "I'll get you back for that."

"Sorry, couldn't resist that one. Anyway, you'll have the flat to yourself tonight. I'm staying at Tom's since we're both on a day off tomorrow."

I shake my head at her.

"You're naughty, Ms Bridge."

"What?" She's trying to look innocent, "I thought you might want to have some privacy so you can talk. That's all I meant." She winks at me.

"I know exactly what you meant, Missy."

I walk to the bathroom and turn on the shower while I'm undressing. I get in and immediately start thinking about Norman Bates. I'm so going to kill her for that. Great! This will happen every time I have a bloody shower now; I know it will.

The same thing happened when I went scuba diving in Egypt. I had a panic attack. I'd only gone down seven metres when I saw a shoal of fish that appeared to be swimming away from me, and then suddenly a theme tune came into my head: *duuuun dun, duuuun dun, dun dun dun dun* ... I closed my eyes, but then had to open them quickly because all I could envisage was a gigantic white shark swimming towards me, its wide-open mouth full of rows of razor-sharp teeth. I turned to see what the fish were swimming away from, because they always say little fish swim away from bigger fish, and caught sight of a black fin. I nearly had a cardiac arrest. The instructor had to swim back to the boat with me. I was hysterical – screaming and spluttering and gasping for my breath. I sat in the boat on my own with the skipper for an hour while everyone else dived. He just rolled his eyes at me, and jabbered away in Arabic. I smiled along, nodding my head, which was daft really, because I'd no idea what he was saying, although I could imagine from the expression on his face: *stupid bloody woman.* So I spent an hour trying my very best not to make eye contact with him, which is difficult on a boat with just the two of you, and far out to sea.

Everyone returned from the dive, and I felt so embarrassed when I realised that the fish were swimming away from me, and that the fin I'd seen was actually my own flipper. I didn't dive again for the rest of the holiday. Instead, I sat on the beach, reading with Gran. I really miss my holidays with my gran.

I finish washing, still laughing at myself, and to my relief the music has stopped playing in my head. I turn off the shower, get out, wrap a large bath towel around myself and walk back to my bedroom.

Alison calls to me, "Do you want me to do your hair?"

"Why not? Thank you! I'll just put something on."

I return to the bathroom in my pyjamas. Alison washes my hair – I'd not yet done it because of the wound on my head. Then she very gently dries it for me too. While she's doing so, I tell her I'm going to move back to the house sometime next week, when I can arrange a locksmith. She offers to come with me if she's not working, and says that if she's on shift she'll stay the night with me.

I thank her, because I don't really want to be in the house on my own, not on the first night back anyway.

We exchange mobile numbers. As I'm entering Alison's into my phone, I notice more text messages from a private number. I know it's almost certainly Adam, so I keep them once again but I don't read them. I know he's stepping up his game, sending me flowers now. He's never done that, not even after the most severe beating, not on birthdays or Christmas. I shudder. Not that I'd want anything at all from him now, apart from a divorce. That's why he's trying to be nice, because he knows he's going to lose everything. So I smile at Alison, forgetting him, and we continue with our little pamper session – doing our nails, having a facial and applying makeup. All that's left for us both to do is to get dressed.

"What are you wearing for your date?" she says.

"It's not a date! It's just drinks and a chat. Anyway, I don't even know where he's taking me."

"Are you dressing up or going casual?"

"I don't know. Do I wear a skirt, trousers or jeans?" I reply, shrugging my shoulders.

"Hmm, let's have a look at what you've brought with you."

I shake my head sceptically.

"I've not brought much at all. I didn't expect to be going out on a date."

She grabs my hand, grinning.

"I knew it was a date!"

I roll my eyes and smile.

"Well, come on. Let's see what I've got."

She pulls me into her room, talking excitedly, barely coming up for air.

"We're about the same size. You're an eight?" She nods without waiting for me to reply, answering her own question.

I follow her into her room, as she starts to rummage

through her wardrobe.

"A dress? Nah. Trousers? Nah. Oh, I know, a nice pair of fitted jeans."

She turns, smiling at me. "Show off that figure of yours. Oh, and this top to go with them. It's sexy, but classy."

She makes me giggle.

"Thanks, Alison."

"Heels?" She throws me a pair of beautiful black strappy shoes.

"I can't borrow these. They're new." I turn them over and see the price tag. A hundred and eighty pounds – they cost a fortune! "Hell, that's more than we earn in a week."

"Of course you can. In fact, I insist," she says, just raising her eyes.

I go off to my bedroom with my new outfit and place the items on the bed. Then I take out my black lace thong and matching bra. I put them on and wriggle into Alison's new ripped skinny jeans, followed by the black top she's given me. It has three-quarter-length sleeves and a cowl neck that falls to my cleavage. It's quite tight in places, especially around my bust. Folds of material cascade down my back to the top of my jeans. It looks classy, although I keep checking in the mirror to see if I can see my bra. It does show slightly, but it's a fancy, strappy bra so it kind of looks like part of the top. There's a knock at my door, and Alison comes in.

"Wow, you look stunning!"

"Don't be daft."

"Trust me, you do. No wonder Edward's pursuing you before anyone else does."

I laugh at her.

"Here, I've brought you a bag."

"Thank you," I say, "and not just for the loan of the clothes, but for everything you've done for me." I give her a hug. "I really do mean it."

She walks out, still wearing her pyjamas. She's not going out until later, as Tom's on a late shift.

I return to the mirror and check my hair and makeup. I hardly recognise myself, although I think I look nice enough for a quiet drink somewhere. Alison's done a fantastic job with my hair. She's done it in soft curls so it falls to one side, hiding the not so attractive dressing on my forehead. The tresses fall over my shoulder and cover my bust, which is a bonus since the top isn't something I would normally wear myself. I look very slim, and rather tall in the expensive strappy heels. I spray on some perfume, then head towards the lounge to wait for Edward.

It's 6.55 p.m. and my tummy is turning over. The palms of my hands are sweating, and my heart is racing. I feel like a schoolgirl on a first date. And then I think how I didn't have a first date at school; Adam was my first.

I pull a face – God, why did I have to think about him? I close my eyes tight and push him immediately from my thoughts. I open them and my thoughts return to Edward. I breathe in, feeling excited but nervous, and stare at the clock: one minute to seven.

My heart has begun to beat faster, as I know I've taken those first steps to break free. And it's a good feeling, a feeling that I'm making my own choices.

I smile as the clock hand hits seven and I hear a knock, heading towards it, nervous, but knowing I'm finally getting my life back as I turn the handle to greet the person behind the closed door.

Book 2 of the Abigail's fate series:
Breaking Free.
Out soon: On Amazon and Kindle.

Acknowledgements

Firstly, I'd like to apologise to my husband and son for being a very grumpy and, at times, almost hysterical wife and mum … sorry!

Secondly, I'd like to thank all my virgin readers for putting up with my tantrums, contrariness and frustration. I know I've driven you all to distraction, but your input and grounding has been invaluable, and this is something I'll never forget. I'm not naming you all individually – you know who you are – but I will say one thing: I'm sorry that you're a little greyer than when we first started this venture together, but, heigh-ho, that's the price of fame!

Lastly, I'd like to thank my mum, without whom these books would not have been possible. She gave me life, laughs and memories, and the courage to be the person I am today.

I cannot believe that I've written four novels. Yes, little old me. Eat your heart out, English teacher. Get in!

So, if you're reading this, thank you so much for buying the Abigail's Fate series. Put your feet up and enjoy her journey towards happiness. If you like it, then rave about it; if you don't, go easy and be kind, because one day you might need a nurse, and, yes, that nurse could be me, waiting around the corner with a big syringe!

Take care and thank you.

Love, Adele x

Printed in Great Britain
by Amazon